W. L. (William Leonard) Courtney

Life of John Stuart Mill

W. L. (William Leonard) Courtney

Life of John Stuart Mill

ISBN/EAN: 9783744664837

Printed in Europe, USA, Canada, Australia, Japan

Cover: Foto ©Raphael Reischuk / pixelio.de

More available books at **www.hansebooks.com**

"Great Writers."

EDITED BY

PROFESSOR ERIC S. ROBERTSON, M.A.

LIFE OF MILL.

LIFE

OF

JOHN STUART MILL

BY

W. L. COURTNEY

LONDON

WALTER SCOTT, 24 WARWICK LANE

NEW YORK : THOMAS WHITTAKER

TORONTO : W. J. GAGE AND CO.

1889

CONTENTS.

———◆———

CHAPTER I.

CHAPTER II.

CHAPTER III.

CHAPTER IV.

CHAPTER V.

CHAPTER IX.

NOTE.

———◆———

IT is needless to say that the following pages are largely indebted to J. S. Mill's *Autobiography*, and to Dr. Bain's two works, *James Mill: a Biography*, and *J. S. Mill: a Criticism*. Besides these, I have found much that was valuable for my purpose in Caroline Fox's *Journals and Letters;* Professor Minto's article in the *Encyclopædia Britannica;* and occasional articles by Mr. Morley in the *Fortnightly Review.* I ought also especially to acknowledge the courtesy of the Right Hon. W. E. Gladstone, who was good enough to write a letter to me on Mill's career in Parliament. To friends who have helped me here and there in the following pages by kindly criticism, I need not offer any public recognition of my gratitude.

OXFORD, *November* 1888.

JOHN STUART MILL.

CHAPTER I.

THE FATHER.

THERE are many points of similarity, as well as of contrast, between the two Mills—father and son—both in character, circumstances, and life. But while in the one case the parentage is an important element, in the other it has, apparently, no appreciable influence. Without James Mill the career of John Stuart Mill is almost inexplicable; but though we know that the father of James Mill was a shoemaker, and that his mother, Isabella Fenton, was a farmer's daughter, it is doubtful whether any stress can be laid on such historical data. There is, as yet, no science of the genesis of greatness. Which of the two men was the more original, and whether both were not men rather of talent than genius, may be considered open questions. James Mill, at all events, was the more consistent thinker. One of the first features in the self-education of John Stuart Mill was the commencement of a revolt against some of the sterner mental discipline which he had imbibed from the teaching and practice of the historian of British India.

It is not easy to rescue the character of James Mill from the depreciation of his enemies, or the laudations of his friends. The more favourable estimate can be perused in the preface which his son wrote to the new edition of the *Analysis of the Human Mind.* " When the literary and philosophical history of this century comes to be written as it deserves to be, very few are the names figuring in it to whom as high a place will be awarded as to James·Mill. In the vigour and penetration of his intellect he has had few superiors in the history of thought : in the wide compass of the human interests which he cared for and served, he was almost equally remarkable : and the energy and determination of his character, giving effect to as single-minded an ardour for the improvement of mankind and of human life as I believe has ever existed, make his life a memorable example. All his work as a thinker was devoted to the service of mankind, either by the direct improvement of . their beliefs and sentiments, or by warring against the various influences which he regarded as obstacles to their progress ; and while he put as much conscientious thought and labour into everything he did, as if he had never done anything else, the subjects on which he wrote took as wide a range as if he had written without any labour at all."* Here, at least, is ungrudging praise ; but the censure, if not equally precise, is, at all events, equally unsparing. " We have been for some time inclined to suspect," says Macaulay in his essay on Mill's article on *Government,* " that these people [the

* Mill's *Analysis.* New Edition (1869). Preface, p. xiii.

Utilitarians], whom some regard as the lights of the world, and others as incarnate demons, are, in general, ordinary men, with narrow understandings and little information. The contempt which they express for elegant literature is evidently the contempt of ignorance. We apprehend that many of them are persons who, having read little or nothing, are delighted to be rescued from the sense of their own inferiority by some teacher, who assures them that the studies which they have neglected are of no value, puts five or six phrases into their mouths, lends them an odd number of the *Westminster Review*, and in a month transforms them into philosophers. Mingled with these smatterers, whose attainments just suffice to elevate them from the insignificance of dunces to the dignity of bores, and to spread dismay among their pious aunts and grandmothers, there are, we well know, many well-meaning men, who have really read and thought much, but whose reading and meditation have been almost exclusively confined to one class of subjects, and who, consequently, though they possess much valuable knowledge respecting those subjects, are by no means so well qualified to judge of a great system as if they had taken a more enlarged view of literature and society."* It is difficult to realise that these are two delineations of the same person. Macaulay, of course, held a brief in this matter, and therefore, if we were compelled to choose between the two verdicts, we should have to accept the less rhetorical estimate ; yet much must be said on the other side, if only to explain the fact that Macaulay's article was one among the other criticisms which induced John

* *Edinburgh Review.* No. 97. March 1829.

Stuart Mill to reconsider and transform the political speculations of his father.

The external events of James Mill's life can be readily summarised. Born in 1773, at Northwater Bridge, in the parish of Logie Pert, county of Forfar or Angus, he was first educated in Montrose Academy, and formed a valuable and life-long acquaintance with Sir John Stuart, of Fettercairn, who eventually gave a name to his eldest son, John Stuart Mill. In 1790 he went to the University of Edinburgh, at the age of seventeen and a half years, and eight years afterwards was licensed as a preacher. It was in 1802 that he, as is not unusual with Scotchmen, turned his back on his native country, and, in the company of Sir John Stuart, entered London. His London life may be divided into three periods. The period of struggle lasts from 1802 to 1819, when he gained an appointment at the India House. From 1819 to 1829 is the time of his greatest and most successful literary activity, the culmination of his career having been reached in 1830. From that time to his death, in 1836, is the period of comparative affluence, when he was not only enjoying the fame of his intellectual work, but had also been made Head Examiner in the India House. But the same period is also one of decreasing energy, due to the gradual decay of his physical powers ; and his death, at the early age of sixty-three, was in large measure caused by the increasing demands which a life of laborious industry had made on his constitution.

The inner life is more important, and requires a longer notice. We have seen that he was originally trained for the ministry, and that he was actually licensed as a preacher. It is not quite clear when he first adopted

the negativist attitude towards religion which he imparted to his son; but the change seems to have been
due to some of the friendships which he formed at an
early period of his life in London, especially the friendship with the South American patriot, General Miranda.*
His chief friends from 1810 onwards were Jeremy
Bentham, Ricardo, Brougham, George Grote, Joseph
Hume, William Allen, the Quaker and philanthropist,
and the radical tailor of Charing Cross, Francis Place.
With all of these he worked in common; most of all,
perhaps, with Bentham. With Bentham he lived in
closest intimacy: he stayed with him both at Barrow
Green and at Ford Abbey, and consoled himself in 1812
with the reflection that if he died, his son would be left
in Bentham's hands. Doubtless he gained from, as well
as imparted to, Bentham's circle of intimate friends
many of those ruling conceptions, both in morals and in
practical life, which were held by the so-called Utilitarian
school; and freedom of thought on religious subjects
would, of course, be included in the intellectual programme. Yet there were discords even in the generally
harmonious relationship with Bentham. We know that
on one occasion Mill had to write a dignified letter to
Bentham, suggesting that it would be better for both
parties if they saw each other less frequently; and though
the breach was temporarily closed, Bentham appears to
have made remarks about his friend in private conversations which, if they were not actually inaccurate, were
certainly ill-natured. He made, for instance, the charge
against Mill's political opinions that they resulted less

---

* So Mill himself told an intimate friend, Walter Coulson. Cf.
Bain's *James Mill*, p. 89.

from love for the many than from hatred of the few—an
opinion which John Stuart Mill indignantly repudiated
on behalf of his father.   Another criticism on his social
demeanour is curious.   " He will never," says Bentham,
" willingly enter into discourse with me.   When he
differs, he is silent.   He is a character.   He expects to
subdue everybody by his domineering tone, to convince
everybody by his positiveness.   His manner of speaking
is oppressive and overbearing.   He comes to me as if
he wore a mask on his face."*   Some of this criticism
is transparently false, for on all sides it was allowed
that Mill was a brilliant conversationalist.   But Lord
Brougham, in the introduction to his speech on Law
Reform (February 7, 1828), in the midst of a general
eulogy on his friend, remarks that " he had something of
the dogmatism of his school ; " and the ' mask on his
face ' receives a pathetic illustration in the comments
which his son afterwards made on his diligent conceal-
ment of a real warmth of feeling towards his children.
There can be no doubt that there was a certain asperity
of manner in his ordinary demeanour, and it served to
mar much of the domestic happiness of his family.   In
1805 he married Harriet Burrow, a girl of unusual
beauty, from whom John Stuart derived his aquiline
type of face ; but, according to Dr. Bain, the union was
never happy, and there was disappointment on both
sides.   A glimpse of the domestic life at Queen's
Square, in 1830, when there was a family of nine, the
eldest twenty-four and the youngest six years of age, fails
to give a pleasing impression.   After John, we are told,

* Quoted from Bowring's *Life of Bentham*, by Bain : *James
Mill*, Appendix, 463.

the next elder children seem to have disappointed their father, and he never looked upon them with complacency. The son speaks of his father as "the most impatient of men," and it is clear that though he could exercise perfect self-control in his intercourse with the world, he did not care to restrain the irritability of his temper at home. The following sentences from Dr. Bain's biography need no comment. "In his advancing years, as often happens, he courted the affection of the younger children, but their love to him was never wholly unmingled with fear, for, even in his most amiable moods, he was not to be trifled with. His entering the room where the family was assembled was observed by strangers to operate as an immediate damper. This was not the worst. The one really disagreeable trait in Mill's character, and the thing that has left the most painful memories, was the way that he allowed himself to speak and behave to his wife and children before visitors. When we read his letters to friends, we see him acting the family man with the utmost propriety, putting forward his wife and children into their due place; but he seemed unable to observe this part in daily intercourse."*

It is pleasant to turn from this side of his character to his intellectual work. His great work, carried out in the midst of pecuniary difficulties and manifold interruptions, was the *History of India*, which was published in 1817, and seems to have secured for him a post in the India House two years afterwards. This was succeeded by the *Elements of Political Economy* in 1821, and a

* Bain's *James Mill*, p. 334.

2

series of most important articles in the supplement to the *Encyclopædia Britannica*, of which the most famous was the one on "Government." It is not too much to say that the essay on Government became the text-book of philosophic radicalism for the whole school of Ben-thamites and Utilitarians, and was in large measure instrumental in that formation of progressive opinion which culminated with the Reform Bill. In 1822 Mill began his chief philosophical treatise, *The Analysis of the Human Mind*, which was not published till 1829. It is an enquiry into mental phenomena on the lines of the English school of Locke and Hume, and is especially remarkable for the use made of Hartley's principle of the Association of Ideas. The next few years witnessed a rapid rise in official position at the India House, and a brilliant series of essays, principally published in the *Westminster Review*. In 1824, he attacked the *Edinburgh* and the *Quarterly* in a couple of articles, which signalised the position of the new democratic school as against the Whigs on the one hand and the Tories on the other. The following year was remarkable for the foundation of the University of London, towards which Mill lent a helping hand, and for a destructive criticism on Southey's *Book of the Church*, in which Mill revealed the width of his divergence from the views of orthodoxy and the ecclesiastical establishment. The *Fragment on Mackintosh* was published in 1835, and offended even his friends by the violence of its attack on Mackintosh's ethical philosophy. An article on the Church and its reform in the *London Review* was succeeded by one on Law Reform in the same periodical. The last year of his life, 1836, was marked by two essays, one on Aristocracy, the other a

dialogue, " Whether Political Economy is Useful," composed in the midst of considerable physical suffering, to
which he succumbed on June 23rd. His career at the
India House had been uniformly successful. Appointed
an assistant to the Examiner of Indian Correspondence, at a salary of £800 a-year in 1819, he
became second assistant in 1821 with a salary of £1000.
Two years afterwards he obtained a further rise to
£1200; a vacancy, which was thus created, leading to
John's appointment as a junior clerk. In 1830 he was
made Examiner, with a salary of £1900, which was
subsequently raised to £2000 on the 17th February,
1836, four months before his death. At their father's
death, all his nine children were alive. The second son,
James, had gone to India with an appointment in the
Civil Service, but the rest were at home, and had been so
almost throughout. None of the children, however, seem
to have been constitutionally strong. The eldest girl,
Wilhelmina, named after Sir John Stuart's daughter,
the heroine of the passion of Scott, died in 1861 ; James
died in 1862 ; Henry, the third son, died of consumption
at Falmouth in 1840 ; while the fourth son, George,
who had entered the India Office, died of disease of the
lungs at Madeira in 1853. "It is apparent," says Dr.
Bain, "that while the father's fine quality of brain was
not wanting in the children generally, John, besides
other advantages, was single in possessing the physical
endurance that was needed for maturing a first-class
intellect."*

The chief characteristic of James Mill is a certain
hardness of fibre, which explains at once his intellectual

* Bain : *James Mill,* p. 334.

success, and the limitations of his character.   In his
political theories, in his studies in jurisprudence and
political economy, in his more abstruse speculations, in
his modes of instruction, in his relations to his friends,
in the daily commerce of his domestic life, in every
sphere and mode of his activity, there is one predominant
spirit, one note which is recurrent through all the diverse
harmonies—the pervading and unmistakable influence
of the eighteenth century.   Cold, inquisitive, and critical,
there is nothing which such a spirit will not analyse,
nothing which it will not dare to comprehend.   Hence,
its clearness, its rationality, its *à priori* method; hence,
too, its unimaginativeness, its want of sympathy, its
essential one-sidedness.   To it the complex motives of
humanity appear simple, because, by an arbitrary
hypothesis, it can reduce them to one primary motive,
the desire for happiness; psychology is all explained by
the theory of association; morals by the principle of the
greatest happiness of the greatest number.   It is the
victim of phrases, of which it ignores the dominion.   It
appeals throughout to experience, and yet its method is
consciously or unconsciously deductive.   The very first
principles from which it deduces are so little axiomatic
that they are just the ones most abundantly controverted.
The reason to which it appeals is that which, because
divorced from the sphere of feeling and passion, instead
of comprehending it in some initial synthesis, is sure to
betray its ultimate impotence.   Half of the instincts of
humanity, poetry and art, religion and literature, remain
for it a sealed book, to be either blindly ignored or
fatally discarded.   Yet within its own realm it is master-
fully lucid and self-sufficient.   It will brook no sophisms,

it will clear away all fallacies, it will admit of no superiors, and if it is not omnipotent, it is because it has undertaken with a single reagent to detect all the elements of a complex universe.

Abundant evidence can be found in James Mill's career of the existence of many of these traits. He was only, perhaps, in some respects an original thinker; in other respects he faithfully reproduced the lineaments of his two great teachers, Hartley and Bentham. Indeed, he somewhat improved on his examples; it was his task to cut the edges more clearly and sharply. Those who have read Hartley's *Observations on Man*, know that he somewhat encumbers his main principle of Associationism by a number of collateral considerations, and enfeebles it by connecting it with a delusive physiological hypothesis of vibrations. In Mill's *Analysis*, the association principle appears in simple and decisive form; he will even "better his instruction," for all modes of association are to be reduced to the single one of contiguity. In Bentham, the utility principle is the key to explain both ethics and politics; it is left to Mill to apply it rigorously to all constitutional forms, and to make a rigidly deductive theory of the one possible government of democracy. In both cases, the logical precision and the analytic excess are equally unfortunate. His attempted simplification of the associative principles in the mind of man to the one case of association by contiguity, is regarded by John Stuart Mill as "perhaps the least successful attempt at a generalisation and simplification of the laws of mental phenomena to be found in the work." Room must, at least, be found for association by means of resemblance, as well as that by means of contiguity. "The attempt to resolve association by resemblance into association by contiguity must, perforce, be unsuccessful, inasmuch as there never could have been association by contiguity without a previous association by resemblance. There is a law of association anterior to and presupposed by the law of contiguity—namely, that the sensation tends to recall what is called the idea of itself, that is, the remembrance of a sensation like itself, if such has previously been experienced."* This is, perhaps, a merely technical point, and, as such, one which could only be significant to the psychologist. Shall we look then at the wider issues involved in Mill's essay on Government? The whole is an *à priori* piece of reasoning, which depends on the following principles. The end of government is the securing of the greatest well-being to the people at large. Now, no one acts against his own interest; therefore, the ends of government are best secured by the people (by means of adequate representation) governing themselves. Monarchy, aristocracy, oligarchy, are necessarily to be condemned. Why? Because in each case the governing body will act for its own interest alone, and this interest in the supposed cases is by no means identical with the interest of the people, but rather opposed and antithetical to it. Such is the rigidly logical framework of Mill's political views. Unfortunately, objection can be made both to its method and some of its practical conclusions. Is the method of political inquiry to be thus strictly deductive? Can we deduce the science of government from the laws of human nature? Can the teaching of actual experience

* Mill's *Analysis*. Edition of 1869, pp. 111, 112. Note by J. S. Mill.

be ignored? One of the most successful parts of Macaulay's criticism on the essay deals with this point. "How," Macaulay asks, "are we to arrive at just conclusions on a subject so important to the happiness of mankind? Surely, by that method which, in every experimental science to which it has been applied, has signally increased the power and knowledge of our species; by that method for which our new philosophers would substitute quibbles scarcely worthy of the barbarous respondents and opponents of the middle ages, by the one method of induction; by observing the present state of the world, by assiduously studying the history of past ages, by sifting the evidence of facts, by carefully combining and contrasting those which are authentic, by generalising with judgment and diffidence, by perpetually bringing the theory which we have constructed to the test of new facts, by correcting or altogether abandoning it, according as these new facts prove it to be partially or fundamentally unsound."* Is this merely the facile rhetoric of a professed opponent? Not so, for when J. S. Mill, in the sixth book of his *Logic*, came to the construction of his science of Sociology, he adopted the same line of criticism in his chapter on the abstract or geometrical method of the interest philosophy of Bentham's school. The cold rationalism of the father has to be corrected by a return to that experience on which his school professed to rely in their logic and metaphysics. Perhaps a more decisive instance can be found in James Mill's essay on Education, which was published, together with the essay on Government, in the supplement to the

* *Edinburgh Review*, March 1829.

Encyclopædia Britannica. And here we cannot do better than quote the opinion of Dr. Bain, who, in most points, sympathises with James Mill. "The *à priori* or deductive handling is here exclusively carried out. The author hardly ever cites an actual experience in education; far less has he a body of experience summed up in empirical laws to confront and compare with the deductions from the theory of the human mind. One would think that he had never been either a learner or a teacher, so little does he avail himself of the facts or maxims of the work of the school."* In such points we can see how the logical mind of the eighteenth-century rationalist failed to correspond to the many-hued panorama of human life, how it produced a picture with clear, hard, positive outlines, which was untouched with the grace of flowing contours, and unsoftened by the changing effects of mist and cloud.

The same hardness of fibre can be seen both in his personal demeanour and in his literary tastes. In his relations to his children and his friends he carefully deprecated all feeling and emotion, as we know by the express declaration of his son. Especially in his attitude to his elder son he seems to have been a hard taskmaster, frequently requiring the infant prodigy to produce bricks without straw. The failure in social relations was, above all, due to the defect of imagination and sympathy—a defect which was exaggerated by his careful avoidance of the lighter literature in his private reading. In his commonplace book, which was presented to the London Library by his son, we find numerous citations from historians, from philosophers, from statesmen, from legal

* Bain : *James Mill*, p. 247.

writers, from theologians; but his reading does not appear to have been extensive in the Belles Lettres, and the few poets to which he does refer he cites for purposes other than the purely literary. We can never imagine him tormenting himself, as his son did during a crisis in his career, with the possible exhaustibility of musical combinations. Still less would he have taken the trouble to write down "Thoughts upon Poetry and its variations," or have appreciated the rising genius of Tennyson, or have attempted to sympathise with Carlyle and Coleridge. His very scepticism is different from ours. He attacks ecclesiastical establishments, and rails against the Church, singling out Laud for an onslaught which equals in fury the subsequent attack on Mackintosh. He began, apparently, by being a Deist, and then, troubled by the moral difficulties of the Divine rule, he became a negationist, pure and simple. But his scepticism was clear and logical, and limited to intellectual issues. It had none of that emotional accompaniment which comes out here and there in J. S. Mill's essay on Theism. It was absolutely devoid of that sense of mystery, and that moral feeling and sympathy for men, which makes so much of the current scepticism of our day sceptical even of itself.

There were other effects, however, of such a temperament as James Mill's on which it would be unjust not to insist. The same hardness of fibre which made him educate his son according to the principles of pure logic, made him also a valuable instrument in the cause of political reform, and a real source of intellectual inspiration among his friends and associates. There can be no question that Mill's writings, both in the *Encyclopædia* and the *Westminster Review*, gave direction and impetus to the Reform movement, which culminated in 1832. It is doubtful whether any other man at this period could have done so great and so valuable service. Macaulay, it must be remembered, had passed through Mill's school, and had been in close contact with Mill's disciples at Cambridge before he advocated the Reform Bill. Moreover, Mill's logical acuteness and practical ability stood him in good stead. He was neither so crotchetty as Cobbett, nor so violent as Orator Hunt, nor did he so wantonly affront his country's feelings as Richard Carlile. Even Bentham could not have sufficed for the crisis without him. In Bentham's Reform Catechism, which was published in 1817, there was an outspoken advocacy of Universal Suffrage. Mill's principles also pointed in the same direction, but he was wise enough to see that there were certain preliminary steps which were indispensable, such as a National Education and the enfranchisement of the middle classes. It is an honourable trait in both the Mills, that though they sympathised to the full with the working classes, they refused to hold out to them delusive hopes—such as the raising of wages by legislation. To the industrial middle class Mill especially appealed, and it was Birmingham and Manchester which secured the passing of the Reform Bill.

Nor had Mill inferior influence in the intellectual than he had in the political world. Here the chief agency was the truly Socratic engine of conversation. Let us listen to Grote's testimony in the article he subsequently wrote on J. S. Mill's *Examination of Sir W. Hamilton:*—"His unpremeditated oral exposition was hardly less effective

than his prepared work with the pen; his colloquial
fertility on philosophic subjects, his power of discussing and of stimulating others to discuss, his ready
responsive inspirations through all the shifts and windings of a sort of Platonic dialogue—all these accom-
plishments were, to those who knew him, even more
impressive than what he composed for the press.
Conversation with him was not merely instructive, but
provocative to the dormant intelligence. Of all persons
whom we have known, Mr. James Mill was the one who
stood least remote from the Platonic ideal of Dialectic—
τοῦ διδόναι καί δέχεσθαι λόγον—(the giving and receiving
of reasons), competent alike to examine others, or be
examined by them in philosophy." The son's tribute is
equally impressive :—" My father," he says in the *Autobiography*, " exercised a far greater personal ascendency
than Bentham. He was sought for the vigour and
instructiveness of his conversation, and used it largely
as an instrument for the diffusion of his opinions. I
have never known any man who could do such ample
justice to his best thoughts in colloquial discussion.
His perfect command over his great mental resources,
the terseness and expressiveness of his language, and the
moral earnestness, as well as intellectual force of his
delivery, made him one of the most striking of all
argumentative conversers. . . . It was not solely, or
even chiefly, in diffusing his merely intellectual convictions that his power showed itself: it was still more
through the influence of a quality, of which I have only
since learnt to appreciate the extreme rarity, that exalted
public spirit and regard above all things to the good of
the whole, which warmed into life and activity every

germ of similar virtue that existed in the minds he came in contact with." The latter lesson was assuredly not lost on the son, and though he was never a conversationalist like his father, no man ever displayed a graver or more sustained devotion to the public good.

CHAPTER II.

"A DISQUISITIVE YOUTH"—(1806–1823).

WHEN Mr. Roebuck came over from America, about 1824 or 1825, to enter the English bar, he called on a relative of his, Thomas Love Peacock, at the India House, where the latter was Examiner of India Correspondence. Mr. Peacock, the friend of Shelley, and himself a poet as well as a novelist, introduced Roebuck to a young man of eighteen, who had but lately become a clerk in the office, and whom he described as "a disquisitive youth." The young man was John Stuart Mill. It is possible to trace some likeness either to Mill, or more probably to his father, in the personage of Mr. MacQuedy, described as a political economist, whom Peacock introduces in his amusing tale of *Crotchet Castle*. For Mr. MacQuedy's name is derived from the letters Q.E.D., and the economist himself would thus figure—with an unmistakable reference to his logical attainments—as "the son of a demonstration."*

* According to a note in an article in the *Quarterly Review* for October 1888 (p. 357), even the incident of Mr. MacQuedy proposing to read his paper after dinner is founded on Peacock's experiences of a dinner with Mill.

Be this as it may, the "disquisitive youth" undoubtedly deserved the description which his senior at the India House gave of him.   He had, despite his youth, inquired very widely in different subjects, and had already attained a very considerable reputation as a writer, a thinker, and a reformer.   He had begun the study of Psychology in the School of Condillac, and continued it in the writings of Locke and Hartley, Hume and Reid. He had perused the history of the French Revolution; he had studied Law with Austin; above all, he had a profound acquaintance with the works of Bentham, through the medium especially of Dumont's *Traités de Législation.*   He had written in the *Traveller* and in the *Chronicle,* as well as in the *Westminster Review.*   He had been much exercised with regard to the Richard Carlile prosecutions for heresy, and had formed an Utilitarian Society at Bentham's house.   Above all, he was known as the son of James Mill, the celebrated historian of India, and the author of that Essay on Government against which Macaulay was afterwards to bring the battery of his rhetoric; and in his own person he was talked about as having been subjected to one of the most extraordinary experiments in education which had probably ever been attempted.

The early education of John Stuart Mill has not yet ceased to be the marvel which it appeared to his own and his father's contemporaries.   In the first place, as he himself remarks in his *Autobiography*, he is "one of the very few examples in this country of one who has not thrown off religious belief, but never had it : I grew up in a negative state with regard to it.   I looked upon the modern exactly as I did upon the ancient religion, as something which in no way concerned me. It did not seem to me more strange that English people should believe what I did not, than that the men I read of in Herodotus should have done so. History had made the variety of opinions among mankind a fact familiar to me, and this was but a prolongation of that fact."* But the Agnostic who is not made but born is not, perhaps, so noteworthy as the youth who acquires the secondary education before he gets the primary. A simple enumeration of Mill's studies in his earlier years is enough to startle the youngest and most ardent of schoolmasters. Some discussion has lately taken place between the Head-Masters of our Public Schools as to the age at which the learning of Greek should begin, and the reformers seem inclined to fix it somewhat later in the school curriculum than has been hitherto the custom. Mill began Greek at the age of three. From his third to his eighth year (at which time Latin was commenced) he principally studied Greek, English, and Arithmetic, and the Greek came first. " My earliest recollection on the subject is that of committing to memory what my father termed vocables, being lists of common Greek words, with their significations in English, which he wrote out for me on cards. Of Grammar, until some years later, I learnt no more than the inflexions of the nouns and verbs, but after a course of vocables, proceeded at once to translation; and I faintly remember going through Æsop's *Fables*, the first Greek book which I read. The *Anabasis*, which I remember better, was the second,"† The following is the list of authors read between 1809 and 1814—that is, between the years of

* *Autobiography,* p. 43.   † *Ibid*, p. 5.

three and eight.   In Greek : Æsop's *Fables*, Xenophon's *Anabasis*, *Cyropædia*, and *Memorabilia*, Herodotus, parts of Diogenes Laertius, part of Lucian, two speeches of Isocrates, and the first six *Dialogues of Plato* (in the common arrangement), from Euthyphro to Theætetus. In English we have principally histories : Robertson, Hume, Gibbon, Watson's *Philip the Second and Third* (his greatest favourite), Hooke's *History of Rome* (his favourite after Watson), Rollin in English, Langhorne's *Plutarch*, Burnet's *Own Time*, the history in the *Annual Register*.   To these, on general subjects, must be added : Millar on the English Government, Mosheim, M'Cree's *Knox*, the voyages and travels of Anson and Cook, *Robinson Crusoe*, *Arabian Nights*, *Don Quixote*, Miss Edgeworth's Tales, and Brooke's *Fool of Quality*.   The Arithmetic was the task of the evenings, and Mill admits that he found it disagreeable.

In his eighth year he began, as has been already said, Latin, and learnt it in conjunction with a younger sister, to whom he taught it as he went on.   Other brothers and sisters were successively added to his list of pupils, though the task of instruction seems to have been especially irksome.   From 1814 to 1818 his chief studies were in Latin, in Greek, and in Mathematics. He mentions, amongst others, the following authors :— Virgil, Horace, Phædrus, Livy, Sallust, Ovid, Terence, Lucretius, Cicero, Homer, Sophocles, Euripides, Aristophanes, Thucydides, Demosthenes, Æschines, Theocritus, Anacreon, Polybius, and, strangest book of all to read at the age of eleven, Aristotle's *Rhetoric*, which his father made him analyse and throw into synoptic tables.   In Mathematics he learnt elementary geometry

and algebra thoroughly, and the differential calculus, and
other portions of the higher mathematics, "far from
thoroughly." In private work, he especially studied
Mitford's *Greece*, having been warned by his father
against its Tory prejudices, and tried to compose a
history of the Roman Government, compiled with the
assistance of Hooke, from Livy and Dionysius. The
last is a significant feature, for what especially interested
him was the struggle between the patricians and
plebeians, in which he enlisted himself as a champion
of the growing democracy. But of other compositions
he does not appear to have been fond. He never
composed at all in Greek, even in prose, and but little
in Latin. He wrote, however, some poetry in the style
of Pope's *Homer*, a book which first revealed to him the
beauty of the Greek epic, and translated into English
metre some of Horace's shorter poems. In English
poetry as such he had no regular education, for his
father disliked the English idolatry paid to Shakespeare,
and only admired Milton, Goldsmith, Burns, and, to
some extent, Spenser. The son added to the meagre
list the poems of Sir Walter Scott, Dryden, Cowper, and
Campbell. The absence of so much of the humaner
studies was compensated for by experimental science.
"I never remember being so wrapt up in any book as I
was in Joyce's *Scientific Dialogues ;*—I devoured treatises
on Chemistry."*

From the age of twelve (1818) a higher course of
study begins, especially Logic and Political Economy.
In Logic, Mill commences with Aristotle's *Organon*, and
reads it to the *Analytica*, profiting little, however, by the

* *Autobiography*, p. 17.

Analytica Posteriora, which belong to a branch of speculation for which he was not yet ripe. Latin treatises on the scholastic logic follow, and a work of much higher order of thought, Hobbes' *Computatio sive Logica*. Mill's practice was to accompany his father in his walks, and to give him a minute account of each day's work, answering his searching questions. The foundations for the first book of his *Logic* were undoubtedly laid in these early promenades. " I well remember how and in what particular walk, in the neighbourhood of Bagshot Heath, [my father] first attempted by questions to make me think on the subject, and frame some conception of what constituted the utility of the syllogistic logic ; and when I failed in this, to make me understand it by explanations. The explanations did not make the matter at all clear to me at the time ; but they were not, therefore, useless—they remained as a nucleus for my observations and reflections to crystallise upon ; the import of his general remarks being interpreted to me by the particular instances which came under my notice afterwards."* Some of the most important dialogues of Plato were read at this time, especially the Gorgias, the Protagoras, and the Republic ; and James Mill's *History of India* was minutely studied. But in 1819 (age thirteen) the new study is Political Economy. Mill's father took him through a complete course on this subject, beginning with daily lectures in his walks, and then introducing his son to the works of Ricardo and Adam Smith.

What judgment are we to form of this remarkable education? It is obvious that we cannot estimate it as

* *Autobiography*, pp. 18, 19.

either bad or good, except in reference to the objects for which it was designed, and the purpose it was intended to fulfil. James Mill wished to educate his son to carry out his own work, to make a thinker after his own likeness, and especially to save his pupil from some of what he deemed the wasteful and unnecessary parts of his own development. The son, therefore, need not go through the same steps as the father, but commence almost at the very point which the older thinker had attained. He must begin by being at once a radical politician, a free-thinker, and a logician. From this point of view, the education was a success ; and Mill may be said, like a second Athene, to have leapt from the head of his father fully armed. But the cost was not inconsiderable, as can be seen from Mill's own admissions in his *Autobiography;* and the father himself must have experienced some disappointment when he discovered later on, in 1826 and onwards, how much his son was destined to differ from himself. It is true that the education at least proved that more can be taught in early years than is commonly thought possible, but there are certain considerations tending to lessen the importance of this result which are worth attention, and which, perhaps, make the experiment a warning rather than an example. In the first place, there does not appear to have been much real affection between the teacher and the pupil, though there was, of course, respectful obedience and loyalty. Mill's own words are decisive on this point. "The element," he says, "which was chiefly deficient in his [the father's] moral relation to his children was that of tenderness. I do not believe that this deficiency lay in his own nature.

He resembled most Englishmen in being ashamed of
the signs of feeling, and, by the absence of demonstration, starving the feelings themselves. If we consider,
further, that he was in the trying position of sole teacher,
and add to this that his temper was constitutionally
irritable, it is impossible not to feel true pity for a father
who did, and strove to do, so much for his children,
who would have so valued their affection, yet who must
have been constantly feeling that fear of him was drying
it up at its source. This was no longer the case later
in life, and with his younger children. They loved him
tenderly; and if I cannot say so much of myself, I was
always loyally devoted to him." This is not otherwise
than a sad picture, especially in the case of a man who
had such singularly fine and strong feeling as John
Stuart Mill himself. An even stronger remark follows,
which throws light on the fact that there was not much
sympathy in the relationship. " I do not believe that
fear, as an element in education, can be dispensed with ;
but I am sure that it ought not to be the main element ;
and when it predominates so much as to preclude love
and confidence on the part of the child to those who
should be the unreservedly trusted advisers of after
years, and, perhaps, to seal up the fountains of frank and
spontaneous communicativeness in the child's nature, it
is an evil for which a large abatement must be made
from the benefits, moral and intellectual, which may
flow from any other part of the education."* Will
it be said that Mill is only making a generalisation
in this passage ? It may be so, but, at least, it is
a generalisation which appears to be prompted by

* *Autobiography*, pp. 51-53.

his own specific experience. For, now and again, he seems to suggest that his father was not very just or reasonable in his demands. When he was trying to learn the higher mathematics, he was continually incurring his teacher's displeasure by his inability to solve problems for which that teacher did not see that he had not the necessary previous knowledge. At the age of thirteen the unhappy boy is expected to be able to define the word "idea," and incurs much displeasure when he naturally fails. And when he is unlucky enough to use the common expression that something was true in theory but required correction in practice, his instructor, trained in Bentham's refutation of Common Fallacies, is highly indignant at what he appeared to think was unparalleled ignorance on the part of a mere child.

Nor can it be doubted that young Mill had to read a great many things which it was impossible that he should understand, and that, therefore, there was actual loss of time in the educational process. He confesses that to read Plato's *Theætetus* at the age of seven was a mistake, which it assuredly was. "But my father, in all his teaching, demanded of me not only the utmost that I could do, but much that I could by no possibility have done." What are we to think of an analysis of Aristotle's *Rhetoric* made by a boy of eleven, or the first four books of Aristotle's *Organon* tabulated in synoptic tables a year later? Can it be imagined that the boy could get any real, rememberable knowledge of so difficult an author at so early a period? It would have been interesting to see the synoptic tables before coming to a conclusion on this matter, but we may perhaps throw some light on it in other ways. At the age of six and a-half, after a considerable course of reading in history, Mill begins to write a history of Rome, which has been, fortunately, preserved by a lady friend of the family. The sketch is very short, equal to about four or five printed pages, but, as Dr. Bain (who quotes from it) remarks,* it shows that his enormous reading had as yet done little for him. In 1820, six years after he had begun Latin, when he was fourteen, he writes a Latin letter to his sisters, which is by no means a fine composition, and which would, perhaps, be surpassed by any clever schoolboy of the same age.† Perhaps a more significant comment on his early education is furnished by his later writings. They do not abound, as we should naturally expect from the enormous mass of literature which he had absorbed, in either direct quotations or those refined allusions to which men of literary attainments and scholars, as a rule, accustom us. On the contrary, they are somewhat poor in this respect. Yet, if ever any man had a chance of showing

---

* Bain : *J. S. Mill*, p. 3.

† The following is the letter in question :—Johannes carissimis sororibus Williaminæ atque Claræ salutem. Credo vos lætaturas epistolæ conspectu: Latine scribo pro vobis in ea linguâ exercendis : Gaudeo à patre audiisse vos in historia Græca vosmetipsas instruere: studium euim illud maxime est necessarium omnibus, seu juvenibus, seu puellis. Mihi condonetis quæso si quem errorem in Latine scribendo feci, quippe semper in nomen Gallicum insido, cum quæram Latinum. Ricardo Doaneo dicatis me non locum in litteris his habuisse, ut illi scriberem ; itaque mihi non irascatur. Scribatis mihi precor, si possitis, Latine, sin minus Anglice. Forte hanc epistolam difficilem ad legendum et traducendum invenietis ; sed vos exercebit. Valeatis. xiii. Kal. Aug. 1820. Vesperi ad hora.—

extensive reading and wide acquaintance with literature, it was John Stuart Mill. But the fact seems to be that memory and culture depend largely on the practice of the imagination in early years. The youthful mind is not very receptive of facts, but is always alive to the imaginative treatment of facts. Plato, in his *Republic*, gives utterance to a striking paradox on this matter. When he is discussing the primary education, he says that instruction must first begin with falsehoods, by which he means mythical tales. Now, the culture of the imagination was a necessity which Mill only recognised later, at the time of his so-called crisis. He makes the remark about his father that he had never sufficiently cared for the concrete illustration of the truths which he desired to instil. "A defect running through his otherwise admirable modes of instruction, as it did through all his modes of thought, was that of trusting too much to the intelligibleness of the abstract, when not embodied in the concrete." If that was so, have we not here an important commentary on the difference between study and knowledge? Of Mill's study we have enough evidence, but of its results we can not be so sure. There is, at all events, some reason for thinking that less application and a larger imaginative exercise might not, perhaps, have produced so precocious a logician, but would possibly have formed a deeper and more consistent thinker. He was aware of this himself when he was talking to Caroline Fox at Falmouth. "This method of early, intense application he would not recommend to others; in most cases it would not answer, and where it does, the buoyancy of youth is entirely superseded by the maturity of manhood, and action is very likely to be merged in reflection. 'I never was a boy,' he said, 'never played at cricket; it is better to let Nature have her own way.'"* "I never was a boy" is the most pathetic reproach that a son can ever address to his father on the management of his youthful years.

But James Mill was too much in earnest with his scheme to care much for letting Nature have her own way. If, as has been said, he wished to make his son a logician and a reformer, he certainly succeeded. The early studies in Aristotle and the school-logic, the early acquaintance with the Socratic method of inquiry, gained by a perusal of the Platonic dialogues, the diligent work of comparing Ricardo with Adam Smith—all bore abundant fruit. The first intellectual operation in which the young Mill arrived at any proficiency was, as he himself says, dissecting a bad argument, and finding in what part the fallacy lay. The Socratic "elenchus," as an education for precise thinking, took such hold of him that it became part of his own mind. "I do not believe," he says, "that any scientific teaching ever was more thorough or better fitted for training the faculties than the mode in which logic and political economy were taught to me by my father. Striving, even in an exaggerated degree, to call forth the activity of my faculties, by making me find out everything for myself, he gave his explanations not before, but after, I had felt the full force of the difficulties; and not only gave me an accurate knowledge of these two great subjects, as far as they were then understood, but made me a thinker on both." The worst of early proficiency, however, is its

* *Journals of Caroline Fox*, i., 163, 164

effects on manners and behaviour. Mill is so entirely
truthful about himself that he himself notices this defect.
He says that various persons who saw him in his childhood
thought him "greatly and disagreeably self-conceited,"
though he does not believe that this was really the case.
He traces the effect on other people to the fact that
he was disputatious, and did not scruple to give direct
contradictions to things which had been said in his
hearing. Doubtless he acquired this bad habit from
having been encouraged in an unusual degree to talk on
matters beyond his age, and with grown persons, while
the usual respect had never been inculcated on him.
It should, however, be added that when he was abroad
with Lady Bentham, she took some pains with his
manners, and that he took her criticisms very well. In
his diary, he remarks that the family of Sir Samuel
Bentham were very kind in constantly, without ill-
humour, explaining to him the defects in his way of
conducting himself in society; for this, he says, " I
ought to be very thankful." But he never was a boy ;
no holidays were allowed him as long as he was under
his father ; he could do no feats of skill in physical
strength, and knew none of the ordinary bodily exercises.
His father saved him, it may be, from the demoralising
effects of school-life, but made no effort to provide him with
any sufficient substitute for its practicalising influences.

The external history of the years up to 1820 was
almost entirely uneventful. Born on May 20th, 1806, in
the house now No. 13 Rodney Street, Pentonville, Mill
lived with his father and his father's friends, Ricardo,
Joseph Hume, and Bentham. At the age of three he
paid his first visit to Bentham at Barrow Green. When

five years old he was taken to see Lady Spencer, whose husband, Lord Spencer, was at the head of the Admiralty, and is said to have kept up an animated conversation with his hostess on the comparative merits of Marlborough and Wellington.   In 1814 his family went to stay with Bentham at his new residence, Ford Abbey, in Somersetshire, and just before this date the two Mills and Bentham made an excursion, which included visits to Oxford, Bath, Bristol, Exeter, Plymouth, and Portsmouth.   The tour had an important result for Mill, for at Gosport he made the acquaintance of Bentham's brother, General Sir Samuel Bentham, at that time superintendent of the Portsmouth Dockyard. Mill was, in consequence, in 1820, invited to visit him and his family (consisting of Lady Bentham, one son, George, and three daughters, all older than Mill) for six months in the south of France, a visit which was ultimately prolonged to nearly a twelvemonth.

Mill wrote a diary of this important event in his early career.   He left London on the 15th May 1820, when he was nearly fourteen, travelled to Paris, where he presented an introduction to M. Say, the political economist, and, as it is pleasant to note any childish incident in so grave a youth-time, played on a hot Sunday (May 21) at battledore and shuttlecock with Alfred Say, the youngest son of the house.   After nine days' stay at Paris, he started by himself to join the Benthams, who were living at a château belonging to the Marquis de Pompignan, a few miles from Toulouse.   Of the journey, which took four days, Dr. Bain gives the following account.*   " Mill makes a blunder in choosing

* Bain : *J. S. Mill*, p. 12.

the cabriolet of the diligence, and finds himself in low company. At Orleans, a butcher, with the largest belly he had ever seen, came in and kept incessantly smoking. On the third day he is at Limoges, and breakfasts in company with a good-natured gentleman from the interior ; but his own company does not much improve ; the butcher leaves, but a very dirty *fille*, with an eruption in her face, keeps up his annoyance. The following day a vacancy occurs in the interior, and he claims it as the passenger of longest standing ; a lady contests it with him, and it has to be referred to the *maire*, the retiring passenger, a young *avocat* pleading his case. He is now in good company, and his account of the successive localities is minute and cheerful. He arrives at his destination at two A.M. the 2nd of June, is received by Mr. George Bentham, and meets the family at breakfast."

The daily record of his life contains his items of work and his experiences in the neighbourhood. He appears to have risen early, worked hard at French, Greek, Latin, and the higher Mathematics ; attempted to learn to dance, sing, fence, and ride, but, as he himself says, without obtaining any proficiency in the latter exercises ; and taken every opportunity of extending his acquaintance with France, the country, the people, and the institutions. One day reads very much like another in the diary of this studious youth. "July 7th. Rose 5¾ ; five chapters Voltaire till 7 ; till 7¼, 46 lines of Virgil ; till 8, Lucian's *Jupiter Confutatus* ; goes on a family errand ; music lesson till 9 ; Lucian continued till 9½, and finished after breakfast at 10¼ ; a call required him to dress ; read Thomson and made Tables till 12¼ ;

seven propositions of Legendre; has him over the coals for his confusion in regard to ratio,—'takes away a good deal of my opinion of the merit of the work as an elementary work;' till 1½ wrote exercises and various miscellanies; till 2½, the treatise on Adverbs; till 3¾, Thomson; *Livre Géographique* and *Miscellanies* till 5; eats a little, dinner being uncertain, owing to a family event; goes for first lesson to music-mistress, a lady reduced by the Revolution, and living by her musical talents; henceforth to practise at her house daily from 11 to 12, and take a lesson in the evening; dined on return, then dancing lesson." The day will serve as a sample for the rest. Mill accompanied the Benthams in an excursion to the Pyrenees, stayed for some time at Bagnères de Bigorre, made a journey to Pau, Bayonne, and Bagnères de Luchon, and ascended the Pic du Midi de Bigorre. He notices himself the impression which this introduction to mountain scenery made upon his receptive mind: "Mais jamais je n'oublierai la vue du côté méridional!" He further went to Montpelier, where Sir Samuel had bought the estate of Restinclière.

Apart from the wider experience gained from this visit to another country, Mill derived other lessons from his stay with the Benthams. He was struck by the difference between the English and French nations, and contrasted their characteristics much to the advantage of the latter. On the one side there was the frank sociability and amiability of French personal intercourse; on the other, there was the English mode of existence, in which everybody else was either an enemy or a bore. He found, it is true, that in France the bad as well as the good points, both of individual and of national character, came more to the surface, and broke out more fearlessly in ordinary intercourse, than in England. But while in France the general habit of the people is to show, as well as to expect, friendly feeling in every one towards every other, wherever there is not some positive cause for the opposite; in England, it is only of the best bred people in the upper or upper-middle ranks that anything like this can be said. From the French society which he saw in Paris in the company of men like M. Say and M. Saint-Simon (the latter of whom he saw but once), he derived his interest in foreign politics, which came out conspicuously in after years. " The chief fruit which I carried away was a strong and permanent interest in Continental Liberalism, of which I ever afterwards kept myself *au courant*, as much as of English politics—a thing not at all usual in those days with Englishmen, and which had a very salutary influence on my development, keeping me free from the error always prevalent in England, and from which even my father, with all his superiority to prejudice, was not exempt, of judging universal questions by a merely English standard."*

Mill returned to England in July 1821, and commenced with ardour the life of a young man of promise, whom his father was understood to have trained after his own model. The two years before his official life was commenced as a clerk in the India House were spent in numerous studies in history and philosophy, and in literary composition. In 1822, for instance, he read up the history of the French Revolution, studied law

* *Mill's Autobiography*, p. 61.

with John Austin (for he was then intended for the bar), perused and deeply admired Dumont on Bentham, worked through much English philosophy, began his intimacy with Grote, and entered the arena of literary life by writing in the *Traveller* newspaper. In the same year, having made acquaintance with many young men resident in Cambridge, who afterwards came to London —such as Macaulay, Hyde and Charles Villiers, Strutt (Lord Belper), and Romilly—he went to Cambridge on a visit to Charles Austin, the younger brother of John Austin. This visit is not alluded to in the *Autobiography*, but Dr. Bain assures us that "the contrast of his boyish figure and thin voice with his immense conversational power, left a deep impression on the undergraduates of the time, notwithstanding their being familiar with Macaulay and Austin." Indeed, Professor Townshend was very anxious to get Mill entered at Trinity College, Cambridge ; but it is equally doubtful whether the father would have consented to this course, or whether the son would have consented to subscribe to the Thirty-Nine Articles. On the 21st of May 1823, however, he was appointed junior clerk in the Examiner's Office at the India House, which effectually precluded other plans for his career.†

* Bain : *J. S. Mill*, p. 28.

† I subjoin some details as to Mill's employment in the India House, taken from Bain's *Life of Mill*. The clerks in those days had no salary, only a gratuity. For three years Mill had £30 a-year ; at the end of that time he received a salary of £100, with an annual rise of £10. In 1828 he was put over the heads of all the clerks, and made an Assistant at £600 a-year, being sixth in rank. In 1830 he stood fifth, his father being at the top. Early in 1836 he gained a step, and on his father's death the same year,

another. He was then third, but David Hill was made second over
his head, Peacock being chief.   His salary was now £1200 a-year,
to which, in 1854, a special and personal addition was made of
£200 a-year.   On March 28, 1856, Peacock and Hill retired
together, and Mill was made Examiner, with a salary of £2000
a-year.   At Christmas 1858, on the transfer of the Company's
government to the Crown, he was superannuated on a pension of
£1500 a-year.

CHAPTER III.

CRISIS—(1823–1840).

THE interest attaching to Mill, not only as a thinker, but as a man, is centred in the fifteen years which succeeded his first entry of the India House. At the commencement of this period he is his father's own son ; at the end of it he has written an article on Bentham, which, by his early friends, was looked upon as almost an apostasy   Amongst the many gifts of Mill's disposition, the greatest, perhaps, was a rare candour and honesty of mind, to which he owes his own somewhat independent position in the ranks of the school to which by inheritance and taste, he belonged. In 1823 he might have been a dogmatist and a bigot ; he seems to suggest, in his Autobiography, that such was the case ; but this was the inevitable intolerance of a precocious youth. He speedily showed himself keenly receptive of influences which came from quarters with which his father could not sympathise, while at the same time he had the moral courage to publish his changing opinions to the world. It is easy, of course, for the critic to point out some of the inconsistencies, begotten of this change, which are to be observed in different parts of his work. It should be no less easy for a biographer to admire that higher inconsistency which is but the synonym of a mental growth—continuous, conscientious, and in the best sense, progressive.

It is necessary to attempt to sketch the position of Mill at the outset of his public career. Democrat, Empiricist, Benthamite, Utilitarian—such terms were, doubtless, the current description of him in the mouth of his contemporaries. We can trace the various features of his character in the successive mental influences which at this time he underwent. In 1822 he first reads the history of the French Revolution. He learns with astonishment that the principles of democracy which in 1822 were in so hopeless a minority everywhere in Europe, had borne all before them in France some thirty years earlier, and had been the creed of the nation. From this time, he tells us, the subject took an immense hold of his feelings. Under the careful training of his father, he had learnt to sympathise with the democracy in Grecian history, and with the struggles of plebeians against the patricians in the annals of Rome ; but here, close to his own era, he found a triumphant vindication of those very principles with which he felt himself allied. The result was a careful study of the French Revolution, and a design to write something on the subject. The literary harvest was not, however, reaped by Mill himself, but by Carlyle, into whose hands Mill seems to have placed a considerable mass of materials. But Mill's own aspirations were now fixed. " What had happened so lately seemed as if it might easily happen again ; and the most transcendent glory I was capable of conceiving was that of figuring, successful or unsuccessful, as a

4

Girondist in an English Convention." The democratic champion was now in the field.

The same year is the real commencement of his philosophic studies. The choice of works bears the unmistakable imprint of the father's guidance. Locke's *Essay on the Human Understanding* is succeeded by Helvetius' *de l'Esprit*, and Hartley's *Observations on Man* is read side by side with James Mill's *Analysis of the Mind*, which at this time is on the stocks. These works are all on that side of philosophic thought which is called Empirical, and contain the main principles of the inductive and experiential scheme. There are no such things as innate ideas ; the mind of man before experience comes is a *tabula rasa*, a blank and characterless piece of paper. How, then, do the successive and fragmentary experiences which come in upon us, through the medium of the senses, crystallise into those abiding thoughts and ideas which we term knowledge? By means of the great mental law of Association, which helps us at once to remember and to reason. Intuition, innate conceptions, a native and *à priori* reason—all these are meaningless terms. There is no innate sense of Duty, or innate idea of God. But such data have been slowly acquired by successive infiltration of experience, and made compact and solid by means of Association. To these principles Mill swore allegiance, and to most of them he remained constant throughout his philosophic career. The method of study was twofold. In private there was the composition of careful abstracts taken from each chapter as he read ; in public there was discussion carried on among friends, either at the house of Bentham or of Grote. The Utilitarian

Society and the Speculative Debating Society were both set on foot at this period, the first in 1823, the second in 1825.

The Utilitarian Society introduces us to a third great influence, perhaps the greatest which Mill recognised, the influence of Bentham. The name itself was a happy piece of nomenclature, which Mill borrowed not from a friend, but an enemy. In one of Galt's novels, *The Annals of the Parish*, a Scotch clergyman, of which the book purports to be an autobiography, warns his parishioners not to leave the Gospel and become Utilitarians. With a boy's fondness for a name and a banner, Mill tells us, he seized on the word, and for some years called himself and others by it as a sectarian application. But the idea which the term was meant to convey was entirely due to Bentham. When Mill was reading Law with Austin his father put in his hands Dumont's *Traité de Législation*, which interpreted Bentham's principal speculations to the Continent. The effect is best described in Mill's own words.* "The reading of this book was an epoch in my life; one of the turning points in my mental history. My previous education had been, in a certain sense, already a course of Benthamism. The Benthamic standard of 'the greatest happiness' was that which I had always been taught to apply—yet in the first pages of Bentham it burst upon me with all the force of novelty. What thus impressed me was the chapter in which Bentham passed judgment on the common modes of reasoning in morals and legislation, deduced from phrases like 'law of nature,' 'right reason,' 'the moral sense,' 'natural rectitude,' and the like; and characterised them

* *Autobiography*, pp. 64-67.

as dogmatism in disguise, imposing its sentiments upon
others under cover of sounding expressions which convey
no reason for the sentiment, but set up the sentiment as
its own reason. It had not struck me before that
Bentham's principle put an end to all this. The feeling
rushed upon me that all previous moralists were superseded, and that here, indeed, was the commencement of
a new era in thought. The impression was strengthened
by the manner in which Bentham put into scientific form
the application of the happiness principle to the morality
of actions, by analysing the various classes and orders
of their consequences. . . . When I laid down the last
volume of the *Traité*, I had become a different being.
The 'principle of utility,' understood as Bentham
understood it, and applied in the manner in which he
applied it through these three volumes, fell exactly into
its place as the keystone which held together the
detached and fragmentary component parts of my knowledge and beliefs. It gave unity to my conceptions of
things. I now had opinions ; a creed, a doctrine, a
philosophy ; in one among the best senses of the word,
a religion ; the inculcation and diffusion of which could
be made the principal outward purpose of a life." There
is no lack here of generous enthusiasm. Nineteen years
later we shall find him almost equally enthusiastic on the
subject of Comte's *Philosophie Positive*.

Mill himself attributes a very large effect to another
influence, which is only so far of interest as it seems
to throw light either by way of contrast or similarity
on his posthumous essays on Religion. He read, at
the suggestion of the elder Mill, a book which was
avowedly written on the lines of Bentham, entitled *The*

Influence of Natural Religion on the Temporal Happiness of Mankind, bearing on its title-page the pseudonym of Philip Beauchamp. It was a discussion of the usefulness of religion rather than of its truth, an inquiry into the effects of belief on the general character and thoughts of mankind at large, without particular reference to any special form of belief except that which might be included under the head of Natural Religion. The conclusion aimed at was an exposure of the hollowness of such Deism as depended on ideas like the course of Providence in history and the physical world. The result on Mill's mind was simply the deepening of what in the fashionable language of the present day would be called his Agnosticism. It was not merely that any form of revealed Religion failed to satisfy him, but that he acquired a conviction that no religion could be founded on what was vaguely termed the teaching of Nature. Some of the elements of so negativist a creed apparently did not appeal to him in later years, for the tone of his last essay on Religion was, as we know, a surprise, and almost a painful surprise, to his friends.

With such influences as we have detailed acting on his mind, and with all the advantages of having as his friends Grote and Austin, to say nothing of a man with so assured a reputation as his father now enjoyed, the young Mill was launched into London society as the champion of the new and philosophical Radicalism. He is known as a trenchant writer in literary organs of advanced thought; he is almost the principal contributor to the new *Westminster Review,* which was started in declared opposition both to the *Quarterly* and the *Edinburgh*; above all, he is the founder and upholder

of societies which aim at the regeneration of the social
fabric by means of Malthus's population principle and
Bentham's greatest happiness of the greatest number.
He is the inspiring spirit of the Utilitarian Society and
the Speculative Debating Society ; while in moments of
leisure he reads and discusses prominent philosophical
works with his friends, and in moments of occupation
attends to the complicated business of the India House.
Such a young man we can readily imagine to figure as a
logical reformer among his associates, and as a revolu-
tionary firebrand among his opponents.   Nor is it hard
to estimate the general character of the youthful band
which surrounded him, either as personal friends or
as satellites.   Anyone who has had any personal
experience of academic debating societies, or of youthful
clubs for the propagation of advanced opinion, can
readily produce in imagination the features of these
reunions.   It may be true that middle-aged men are
cynics ; it is abundantly true that young men are
doctrinaires.   All the good side of adolescent energy
goes to the production of such societies—its warmth of
feeling, its confident logic, its boundless self-reliance,
together with that serene indifference as to the relation
of extreme theory to ordinary practice which constitutes
at once the charm and the prodigal wastefulness of
juvenile speculation.   We can imagine the perfervid zeal
of Charles Austin, on whose shoulders even Mill places
the blame for such poor estimate as Benthamism enjoyed
in the world ; and we can sympathise with, though Mill
invites us to smile at, that determination to *outrer*
whatever was by anyone considered offensive in philosophical radicalism, which was the badge and emblem of

the members of the coterie. Meanwhile there was abundant cleverness in the ranks, though perhaps not so much identity of principles as the world gave them credit for. But it was not long before Mill discovered that sectarianism was foolish. Indeed, he records the usual fate of such societies when he remarks of the one which he championed, that all who had anything in them quickly outgrew their boyish vanity, and those who had not, became tired of differing from other people, and gave up alike the good and the bad of the heterodox opinions they had professed.*

Carlyle spoke of Mill to Caroline Fox with that magisterial scorn mixed with shrewd penetrative insight which he generally employed in his judgments : " Ah, poor fellow! he has had to get himself out of Benthamism ; and all the emotions and sufferings he has endured have helped him to thoughts that never entered Bentham's head. However," he continues, " he is still too fond of demonstrating everything. If John Mill were to get up to heaven, he would be hardly content till he had made out how it all was. For my part, I don't much trouble myself about the machinery of the place ; whether there is an operative set of angels, or an industrial class, I'm willing to leave all that."† This was a far better criticism than a previous judgment of Carlyle, when he exclaimed, on reading some of Mill's earlier writings, " Here is a new mystic ! " For it serves to illustrate from the outside those touching self-revelations which Mill has put in the fifth chapter of his *Autobiography.* What Mill calls " a crisis in my mental

* *Autobiography*, p. 79.
† *Journals of Caroline Fox*, i. 309.

history " began in 1826. The year before, when he was
only nineteen, had been passed in remarkably laborious
industry. His principal occupation had been the editing
of Bentham's book on Evidence. His subsidiary work,
quite apart from his official duties as clerk, runs as
follows :—*Parliamentary History and Review* started.
Writes the following articles—on Catholic Disabilities,
on the Commercial Crisis, on Currency, and on the Reci-
procity Principle in Commerce. Learns German. Begins
morning readings in the Utilitarian Society at Grote's
house in Threadneedle Street. Goes with some others
to the debates of the Owenites' Co-operative Society.
Founding of the Speculative Debating Society. Writes
in the *Westminster* on the Political Economy of the
Quarterly, on the Law of Libel (?), and on the Game
Laws (?) [number for January 1826]. Here was a list
which was enough to tax even so untiring a brain as
Mill's. Yet, perhaps, it is a prosaic opinion to attribute
the mental crisis, as Dr. Bain does, principally to
physical causes and to the overworking of the brain.
Mill treats his malady almost entirely on the subjective
side, and that he passed through some kind of a spiritual
crisis can hardly be doubted by anyone who studies its
sequel in the altered tone of his later writings. Carlyle
was undoubtedly right, he had to get himself out of Benthamism ; and the process was rendered doubly difficult
and painful owing to the respect and admiration he
entertained for the Benthamism of his father. When
the light of newer thoughts breaks upon cherished
opinions, a mental tragedy, which is by no means the
less real because it is subdued, makes havoc of a man's
peace and self-control.

Mill's own graphic account of himself at this period has often been quoted, but will bear quoting again as a most interesting piece of psychological analysis :—" I was in a dull state of nerves, such as everybody is occasionally liable to, unsusceptible to enjoyment or pleasurable excitement : one of those moods when what is pleasure at other times becomes insipid or indifferent ; the state I should think in which converts to Methodism usually are when smitten by their first ' conviction of sin.' In this frame of mind it occurred to me to put the question directly to myself :— ' Suppose that all your objects in life were realised, that all the changes in institutions and opinions which you are looking forward to could be completely effected at this very instant, would this be a great joy and happiness to you ? ' And an irrepressible self-consciousness distinctly answered, ' No ! ' At this my heart sank within ; the whole foundation on which my life was constructed fell down. All my happiness was to have been found in the continual pursuit of this end. The end had ceased to charm, and how could there ever again be any interest in the means ? I seemed to have nothing left to live for."

This is the shipwreck of Rationalism, at least of that narrow and poverty-stricken Rationalism which was the boast of the eighteenth century. The end of life, both for the individual and for the community, is happiness. Everything, whether health, or money, or virtue itself, exists as a means to this sovereign end. The office of reason, then, is to adapt these means, to work them out by chains of calculation and argument, to make them fall into their proper subordination and value, as viewed in the light of this universal end. But happiness is the gift of emotional, expansive characters, and not of calculating machines; to aim at happiness in every act or project is, as common experience shows, the very way to lose it. A man is not a logical engine; he is a complex of feeling and reason, and the emotional elements within him will not be mulcted of their rights. Dwarf the feelings, starve the artistic instincts, eradicate the moral sentiment, and the result will be a barren sacrifice, a suicidal victory, which is only fortunate when it does not mean an anarchic revolt. The teaching of the older Mill had been throughout the suppression of feeling; the watchword of the Utilitarian Society had been the continual outcry against innate sentiment. Bentham had not hesitated to malign all poetry as misrepresentation, and vindicate the claim of pushpin as a quantitative equivalent to Milton and Shakespeare; and the issue is seen in John Mill sitting down in despair, with all his schemes of life and human regeneration lying in ruins around him.

Such a crisis is not wholly uncommon, but its issues will differ with different men. In one man's case it will lead to the resignation of earlier ideals, as when Plato, after writing the *Republic*, is led by his actual experiences in Sicily to write *The Laws*. In the case of another man, it will issue in an unworthy cynicism, as when Tourguénef, after his dream in *Pères et Fils* had gained a realisation in the emancipation of the serfs in 1860, sat down to write those sallies of a disappointed idealist which we find in *Fumée* in 1868. Rarely enough do we find the crisis issuing in an enlargement of view, as was the case with Mill. There can be no doubt how the

larger lessons were first brought home to his mind. In
the Speculative Debating Society he had come across
Frederick Maurice and John Sterling, and the new
impression seems to have effaced the influence of
Charles Austin. Here were men who had themselves
a Radicalism of their own, but it was not the Radicalism
of Bentham. What was the secret of their lives? How
had they preserved their souls alive amid the arid fields
of utility and selfishness? By what course of study or
sympathetic communing with alien minds had they
refused to bow the knee to the greatest happiness
principle? And the answer seemed clear. They would
have nothing to say to sectarianism; they thought self-
culture a duty, and they read Wordsworth and Coleridge.
They were not fond of analytic habits, they were
sceptical of the enormous value of Hartley's Association
principle, and they did not believe that happiness was
the sole end. "Analytic habits," says Mill, with
plaintive emphasis, "are a perpetual worm at the root
both of the passions and of the virtues." It was a
notable discovery, for it cast some doubt on his own and
his father's metaphysics, and suggested that we must take
happiness by the way, by pursuing some given end
without reference to this so-called universal standard.
And so Mill, in the autumn of 1828, begins for the first
time to read Wordsworth, and turns his thoughts in the
direction of Carlyle, Goethe, and Coleridge.

The articles which Mill wrote in the ensuing years
are the best evidence of the reality of his change. As
is the case with all cautious men, the change worked
slowly. But it was unmistakable to his friends. When
Mill became editor of the *London Review*, Mrs. Grote

wrote to Roebuck (April 1837)—"I am quite persuaded the *Review* will cease to be the engine of propagating sound and sane doctrines on Ethics and Politics under J. M. Whether, by getting hooks baited with carrion, he attracts other sorts of fish than those *we* angle for, and thus render it a better investment, I really am not in a condition to judge. But, on the other hand, it is a matter of entire indifference to me so viewed. For my part, I only wonder how the people contrive to keep improving under the purveyance of the stuff and nonsense they are subjected to."* Mrs. Grote is, no doubt, unnecessarily venomous here, but Dr. Bain admits that there was, for some time, an alienation between Mill and his old friends. Mill was still a reformer and an Utilitarian, but he wore his rue with a difference. The chief points in his change of attitude we have now to see.

Characteristic materials are to be found in some of the essays which were deemed worthy of being preserved in the *Dissertations and Discussions* — especially the articles on Bentham and Coleridge contributed to *The London and Westminster*, 'Thoughts on Poetry,' and 'Alfred de Vigny,' the first of which was published in the *Monthly Repository*, the second in *The London and Westminster*, and the paper on De Tocqueville, by means of which Mill made his *début* in the pages of the once hotly-attacked *Edinburgh*. It was the Bentham article which seems to have given offence, for it revealed an attitude towards the oracle which was rather that of the critic than of the disciple. Such sentences as the following, for instance, were not calculated to propitiate

* Quoted by Bain. *J. S. Mill*, p. 56, note.

his friends :—" Bentham's lot was cast in a generation of the leanest and barrenest men whom England has as yet produced, and he was an old man when a better race came in with the present century." " He saw in man little but what the vulgarest eye can see ; recognised no diversities of character but such as he who runs may read." "No one, probably, who in an instructed age ever attempted to give a rule to all human conduct, set out with a more limited conception either of the agencies by which human conduct *is,* or of those by which it *should* be, influenced."* If the merit of Bentham is that he was the father of innovation, the great subversive and critical thinker of his age, and the founder of a method which has many of the best elements of inductive science, his defects are equally obvious and striking. He failed principally in that he was unable to derive light from other minds ; and the inability was rendered the more striking owing to the singular incompleteness of his own mind. The two defects hang together, for the power of learning from others is due to an assimilative faculty, be it sympathy, or imagination, in which Bentham was curiously deficient. The result is that his picture of humanity, like that drawn by an earlier thinker with whom he has some affinity, Thomas Hobbes, is wanting in some of the chief elements which are characteristic of the species. To describe a man as a being moved by self-love, and susceptible only of the stings of pain or pleasure, is to leave out all the higher motives, to narrow down sympathy to its simplest and barest form, and to translate disinterestedness into the calculating desire for general happiness. All, therefore, that Bentham's philosophy

* Mill : *Dissertations and Discussions,* vol. i., p. 355, etc.

can do for the individual is to prescribe some of the
more obvious dictates of prudence, or outward probity, or
beneficence.   It can not help him in what Mill had now
discovered to be one of the chief agencies, not only of
personal happiness, but of success in the highest sense
of the word ; it can not help him in the formation of his
own character ; it can suggest no consistent mode of
self-culture.   Nor can it do much more for society at
large.   It can, indeed, teach the means of organising and
regulating the merely *business* part of the social arrangements ; and, hence, we can understand Bentham's success
in the reform of Law.   But national character, its importance, and the width of its range, the key it furnishes for
the solution of historical problems, and the necessity for
its recognition by the political reformer—all this is for it
a sealed book, owing to the poverty of its psychological
and historical groundwork.   Is his theory of Government
more successful ?   According to Bentham, government
is the authority of the numerical majority ; to give more
political power to the majority is the essence of so-called
Radicalism, whether professed by Bentham himself, or
illustrated in James Mill's essay on Government.   But
there are limits to the authority of the majority.   It
should always respect the personal liberty of the
individual, and it should always show deference to the
superiority of cultivated intelligence.   To Mill, at all
events, these were cardinal maxims, enforced in his
later years, not only by his essay on Liberty, but also
by his efforts in Parliament to secure some sort of
representation for minorities.   Perhaps, too, with respect
to the utility principle, Bentham was wrong in empha-
sising it out of all regard to those secondary principles

and ends which move the greater portion of mankind. It might, indeed, be urged that this only proved an excess of logical and rational principle, without which there could be no rational philosophy. Yet it must also be admitted that there are other modes of regarding actions than their purely moral aspect. There is the æsthetic aspect, for example, which finds such abundant illustration in the creations of art—in music, in poetry, in the drama. On this side, Bentham's limitations are notorious. Nor could he see how the artistic and emotional instincts enter even into the sphere of morals. "His ignorance of the deeper springs of human character prevented him (as it prevents most Englishmen) from suspecting how profoundly such things enter into the moral nature of man, and into the education both of the individual and of the race."* If Mill could utter such criticisms, we can understand the humaner, if less consistent, version which he propounded some years later, of the doctrines of Utilitarianism. This discovery of Bentham's limitations in the æsthetic department was closely connected with Mill's newer studies in poetry. In the midst of his own desolation, when he found that life contained for him no objects to live for, Mill turned, as he tells us, to Wordsworth, and found in his poems a real medicine for his mind. The reason was that these poems expressed states of feeling, and of thought coloured by feeling, under the excitement of beauty. They seemed to be the very culture of the feelings of which he was in quest. It was true that Wordsworth, compared with the greatest poets, "might be said to be the poet of unpoetical natures, possessed of quiet and contemplative

* *Dissertations and Discussions*, vol. i., p. 389.

tastes. But unpoetical natures are precisely those which require poetic cultivation ; and this cultivation Wordsworth is much more fitted to give than poets who are intrinsically far more poets than he." From Wordsworth Mill went on to Shelley, and, struggling as he was against a nature essentially logical, he was able to appreciate a nature which was so diametrically opposed to his own. Indeed, in his *Thoughts on Poetry*, he even exaggerates the importance of the emotional element as entering more exclusively into the character of the true poet than the intellectual. The highest form of poetry appeared to him to be the lyrical, where the musing of the poet is not so much heard as overheard. He draws a distinction between the poet of culture, like Wordsworth, and the poet of emotion, like Shelley ; and, carried to the farthest point by the reaction against his previous forms of thought, he estimates Shelley as much the finer poet of the two. " The state of [poetic] feeling may be either of soul or of sense, or oftener (might we not say invariably ?) of both ; for the poetic temperament is usually, perhaps always, accompanied by exquisite senses. Whatever of sensation enters into the feeling must not be local or consciously organic ; it is a condition of the whole frame, not of a part only. States of feeling, whether sensuous or spiritual, which thus possess the whole being, are the fountains of that which we have called the poetry of poets."* Poetry is found to emanate from a mental and physical constitution, peculiar, not in the kind, but in the degree of its susceptibility ; a constitution which makes its possessor capable of greater happiness than mankind in general, and also of greater unhappiness ;

* *Dissertations and Discussions*, vol. i., p. 87.

and, because greater, so also more various. "Such poetry, to all who know enough of nature to own it as being in nature, is much more poetry, is poetry in a far higher sense than any other." Assuredly such sentiments as these are far enough removed from the Benthamic stand-point. Nor will Mill refuse to adopt as his own the views which Alfred de Vigny puts in the mouth of his hero, Stello. If asked why he felt himself to be a poet, the answer he gives is one which Mill is prepared to endorse—"Because there is in nature no beauty, nor grandeur, nor harmony, which does not cause in me a prophetic thrill—which does not fill me with a deep emotion, and swell my eyelids with tears divine and inexplicable. Because of the infinite pity I feel for mankind, my companions in suffering, and the eager desire I feel to hold out my hand to them and raise them incessantly by words of commiseration and of love."* It was by sympathy with such emotional ardours as these that Mill's own nature was becoming exalted and enlarged.

We can now understand why Mill could feel an interest even in the reactionary and conservative elements to be found in Coleridge. Nothing is more remarkable in Mill than his sudden awakening to the fact that there must be a party of order as well as a party of progress. Theoretically, he discovered that the line of advance in history was spiral rather than rectilineal; in practice he from this time was fond of maintaining that the truth lay somewhere between the views of two counterbalancing and antagonistic parties. The French *philosophes* had made a great error in thinking that

* *Dissertations and Discussions*, vol. i., p. 323.

they could make a clean sweep of society and of the Church. The historical and philosophic views of Coleridge and the Germans were much truer. For the stability of society depends not only on a large system of national education, but also on a feeling of allegiance or loyalty to some principle or set of principles. A necessary condition is that there must be something which is settled, and not to be called in question. "Grote never ceased to convert this remark into an expression for the standing intolerance of society towards unpopular opinions," says Bain;* a comment which shows clearly enough how far Mill had drifted from his old anchorage. But Sectarianism in its narrower forms was henceforth impossible for Mill. "J'ai trouvé que la plupart des sectes ont raison dans une bonne partie de ce qu'elles avancent, mais non pas tant en ce qu'elles nient."† The more he studied Continental thought, the more he was disposed to qualify that absolute value of Democracy for which his father contended. This comes out very clearly in his essay on De Tocqueville's *Democracy in America.* There is such a thing as a tyranny of the majority, and manhood suffrage might conceivably fasten its fetters more closely. There ought to be a learned class, there ought to be even a leisured class. "The sure, and now no longer slow, advance by which the classes hitherto in the ascendant are merging into the common mass, and all other forces giving way before the power of mere numbers, is well calculated to inspire uneasiness even in

---

* Bain : *J. S. Mill*, p. 57.

† *Dissertations and Discussions*, i., 458.   " I have found that most sects are right in a good part of what they advance, but not so right in what they deny."

those to whom democracy *per se* presents nothing alarm-
ing. It is not the uncontrolled ascendency of popular
power, but of any power, which is formidable. There is
no one power in society, or capable of being constituted
in it, of which the influences do not become mischievous
as soon as it reigns uncontrolled—as soon as it becomes
exempted from any necessity of being in the right by
being able to make its mere will prevail without the condition of a previous struggle. To render its ascendency
safe, it must be fitted with correctives and counteractives,
possessing the qualities opposite to its characteristic
defects.* The general result of these considerations on
Mill's political theories may be seen partly in the sixth
book of his *Logic*, partly in the pages in the *Autobiography*,
where he sums up his newer stand-point. In the *Logic*
he has much to say on the proper method of political
science. It must not be empirical, as though its subject-
matter was like the data with which Chemistry deals,†
nor yet geometrical, or abstract, as though it could all be
deduced from some general principle, such as the utility
principle of Bentham. But it must be either deductive
like the method of physical science in its discovery of
causes, or deductive in the sense in which Comte propounded his historical method in the *Philosophie Positive*.
In the *Autobiography* he speaks of the influence on
himself of the St. Simonians, Bazard and Enfantin, and
discovers that their criticisms on the common doctrines
of Liberalism are full of important truth. He was,

---

* *Dissertations and Discussions*, vol. ii., p. 80.

† Macaulay's attack on his father's "Government" article,
declared that the only method of Political Science was experimental
and inductive.

indeed, still a Radical and a Democrat for Europe, and especially for England.   What he altered was the premises of his political philosophy.   He learnt to look upon the device of political institutions as a moral and educational question more than one of material interests.   He ceased to consider representative democracy as an absolute principle ; and took the truer view that it was a question of time, place, and circumstance.   But, on one point, he went further than the Liberals and Democrats of his age. In 1831 Mill was first introduced to Mrs. Taylor.   Perhaps it is not fanciful to trace to this acquaintance the commencement or, at anyrate, the deepening of his convictions as to the justice of Female Suffrage, and the absolute equality of men and women.   Speaking of the St. Simonians, he says, " I honoured them most of all for what they have been most cried down for—the boldness and freedom from prejudice with which they treated the subject of family, the most important of any, and needing more fundamental alterations than remain to be made in any other great social institution, but on which scarcely any reformer has the courage to touch.   In proclaiming the perfect equality of men and women, and an entirely new order of things in regard to their relations with one another, the St. Simonians, in common with Owen and Fourier, have entitled themselves to the grateful remembrance of future generations."

* *Autobiography*, pp. 167, 168.

CHAPTER IV.

"A SYSTEM OF LOGIC"—(1840-1843). ·

THE ten years between 1830 and 1840 were for Mill full of numerous incidents and toils. A visit to Paris after the Revolution of July in 1830 renewed his keen interest in French politics, and made him for several years a diligent student of French affairs. Of his writings from 1832 to 1834 he made the remark, that even if the newspaper articles were left out, they would make a large volume. His father's death in 1836 was succeeded by an illness, which caused a three months' absence in Switzerland and Italy. Another illness followed in 1839, and a second and a longer absence of six months in Italy. He recovered slowly from both attacks, but the first, which seems to have been an affection of the brain, left its mark on him in an almost ceaseless twitching over one eye. The main work, however, for which he was slowly preparing himself during these years, was *The System of Logic*, which was not published till 1843. The first foundation was, perhaps, laid in the readings on logical subjects, which took place in Grote's house when he was twenty-one years of age. At the same date he composed an article on Whateley's *Logic*, which was published in the *West-minster Review.* Then, in 1830, we find him putting on paper some ideas on Logical Distinctions among Terms, and the import of Propositions, followed in 1831 by a consideration of Logical Axioms and the Theory of the Syllogism.   A long interval ensues, in which he is grappling with the problems of Induction, and the pro-cedure of Science, which are to occupy the third book of his *Logic*, and of which he seems to have made a rough draft in 1838.   Further problems, dealing with Sociology and the Logic of the Moral Sciences, are discussed and solved in 1840, when the work is temporarily completed by what afterwards is called the sixth book.

It was in 1840 that his brother Henry was dying of consumption at Falmouth, nursed by Mrs. Mill and her two daughters, Harriet and Clara ; and on March 16th he was visited by John, who stayed with him till his death on April 4th.   It was at Falmouth that Miss Caroline Fox first made the acquaintance with Mill which she has so charmingly related in her *Journals.**   As we have here several noticeable passages of description, we may well linger for a little over her sympathetic pages, especially as fortune had thrown her in the way of many of the eminent men of her time, and thus furnished her with a standard of judgment admirably acute and valu-able.   The way is prepared for her reception of Mill by an enthusiastic account of him by John Sterling, who was one of the firmest friends of the Fox family.   Nor is she disappointed when she sees him.   He is a very uncommon-looking person, she remarks ; such acuteness and sensibility marked in his exquisitely chiselled

* *Journals of Caroline Fox.*   Edited by Horace N. Pym.   2 vols.

countenance, more resembling a portrait of Lavater than any other that she remembers. His voice is refinement itself, and his mode of expressing himself tallies with voice and countenance. She also notices his " wonderfully keen, quiet eyes." With this we may compare a somewhat cooler picture drawn of him by Dr. Bain, when he saw him at the India House two years later, in 1842. "The day after arriving (in London), I walked down to the India House, and realised my dream of meeting Mill in person. I am not likely to forget the impression which he made upon me as he stood by his desk, with his face turned to the door as we entered. His tall, slim figure, his youthful face and bald head, fair hair and ruddy complexion, and the twitching of his eyebrow when he spoke, first arrested the attention; then the vivacity of his manner, his thin voice approaching to sharpness, but with nothing shrill or painful about it, his comely features and sweet expression, would have all remained in my memory, though I had never seen him again. To complete the picture, I should add his dress, which was constant, a black dress-suit, with silk necktie. Many years after that he changed his dress-coat for a surtout; but black cloth was his choice to the end."* That he had made a pleasant impression on the little Falmouth circle Mill was quite aware, for he was the recipient of many acts of kindness; but he made a characteristic remark in a letter to Caroline's brother, R. Barclay Fox—"You have not, nor have even those of your family, whom I have been so fortunate as to see more of, as yet seen *me*, as I really and naturally am, but a *me* artificially made, self-conscious, egotistical, and

* Bain : *J. S. Mill*, p. 64.

noisily demonstrative, by having much feeling to show, and very little time to show it in." Perhaps Mill, like so many other men of talent, was deficient in (and deplored the deficiency of) the winning gift of naturalness.

There are many points of interest brought out in Caroline Fox's *Journals*. Not the least interesting is the light thrown on the friendship between Mill and John Sterling. Sterling was himself the intimate friend of Coleridge, Maurice, and others who, like Dr. Calvert (to whom there are many allusions in the *Journals*), represented a very different side of thought and life from that with which Mill was in early years familiar. The first acquaintance is alluded to,—a hard fight at the Debating Society at Cambridge, when Mill appeared as a Benthamite and Sterling as a Mystic; since that time the two antagonists approximated to one another more and more. It is not difficult to understand in what way they supplemented each the other's gifts and defects. To Sterling, Mill appeared "the most scientific thinker extant, more than Coleridge was, more continuous and severe;" on the other hand, he was deficient in the range of poetical feeling, because he had "singularly little sense of the concrete." To Mill, on the contrary, Sterling was the man who had taught him to read Wordsworth, and who had first suggested to him the necessity of a culture of the emotions. He is, therefore, pleased to make Sterling and the Fox family known to each other, because he is sure they will be full of mutual appreciation: and Miss Caroline Fox adds, "he talked enthusiastically about him." Nor is the change which is going on within Mill unknown to his sympathetic critics at Falmouth. "No one," said Mill to Miss Fox, "should attempt anything intended to benefit his age without at first making a stern resolution to take up his cross and to bear it. If he does not begin by counting the cost, all his schemes must end in disappointment ; either he will sink under it as Chatterton, or yield to the counter-current like Erasmus, or pass his life in disappointment and vexation as Luther did." Miss Fox quite understood that these words contained a personal allusion. It was evidently a process through which the speaker himself had passed, as was sufficiently attested by his care-worn and anxious, though most beautiful and refined, countenance. Sterling supplies the explanation. He had been trained by his father in the strictest sect of Bentham, and was slowly emancipating himself by turning to Wordsworth and Coleridge. Sterling spoke of the gradual development which he had watched in him. "He has made the sacrifice of being the undoubted leader of a powerful party for the higher glory of being a private in the army of Truth, ready to storm any of the strong places of Falsehood, even if defended by his late adherents. He was brought up in the belief that politics and social institutions were everything, but he has been gradually delivered from this outwardness, and feels now clearly that individual reform must be the groundwork of social progress." Caroline Fox learns the same facts in a negative fashion from the lips of Dr. Bowring, Bentham's literary executor. In a visit which Bowring paid to Falmouth, on August 7th, 1840, he spoke of Mill " with evident contempt as a renegade from philosophy, *Anglicè*, a renouncer of Bentham's creed and an expounder of Coleridge's. S. T. Coleridge's mysticism Dr. Bowring never could understand, and characterises much of his teaching as a great flow of empty eloquence, to which no meaning was attachable. Mill's newly-developed 'Imagination' puzzles him not a little; he was most emphatically a philosopher, but then he read Words-worth, and that muddled him, and he has been in a strange confusion ever since, endeavouring to unite poetry and philosophy."

Indeed, many softer touches appear in Mill's char-acter, as seen by the kindly glance of Caroline Fox and her Falmouth friends. Death, the great leveller, had brought the philosophic and the religious mind into nearer relationship, and Henry's last hours inspired many new and strange interests. It is a new thing, said Sterling, for John Mill to sympathise with religious characters, for some years ago his father had made him quite a bigot against religion. And there is a pleasant picture of Dr. Calvert and John Mill standing one on one side, the other on the other of Henry's death-bed. Dr. Calvert remarked, "This sort of scene puts an end to Reason, and Faith begins;" the other emphatically answered "Yes," and a conversation ensued "which displayed much humility and deep feeling." The fol-lowing sentences from a letter which Mill wrote to Barclay Fox are not the language we might have expected from the man who was regarded as one of the sceptics of his age. "I know not how dangerous may be the ground on which I am treading—but surely a more Christian-like interpretation of the mystery of the Atonement is that which, believing that divine wisdom punishes the sinner for the sinner's sake, and not from an inherent necessity more heathen than the heathen

Nemesis, holds, as Coleridge did, that the sufferings of the Redeemer were (in accordance with the eternal laws on which this system of things is built) an indispensable means of bringing about that change in the hearts of sinners, the want of which is the real and sole hindrance to the universal salvation of mankind." Perhaps, too, no apology is needed for reproducing in a foot-note the Calendar of Odours which Mill made for Caroline Fox. We are so soon to regard Mill in the colder aspect of logician, that we may be pardoned for lingering on that sunnier aspect which he wore for his young Quaker friend.* Mill was throughout his life an enthusiastic botanist; and three days before his death he walked fifteen miles on a botanical excursion.

Meanwhile, during all these years, despite his literary labours as editor of the *London Review* (of which Sir W. Molesworth was proprietor), despite his two illnesses,

---

* "A Calendar of Odours, being an imitation of the various Calendars of Flora by Linnæus and others.

"The brilliant colouring of Nature is prolonged with incessant changes from March till October; but the fragrance of her breath is spent before the summer is half ended. From March to July an uninterrupted succession of sweet odours fills the air by day, and still more by night; but the gentler perfumes of autumn, like many of the earlier ones here for that reason omitted, must be sought ere they can be found. The Calendar of Odours, therefore, begins with the laurel and ends with the lime.

" *March.*—Common laurel.

" *April.*—Violets, furze, wall-flower, common broad-leaved willow, apple-blossom.

" *May.*—Lilac, night-flowering stocks and rockets, laburnum, hawthorn, seringa, sweet-briar.

" *June.*—Mignonette, bean-fields, the whole tribe of summer roses, hay, Portugal laurel, various species of pinks.

and his increasing work as he rose in the employ of the India House, the *Logic* was growing apace. Dr. Bain helped him with instances of induction in the third book, and Auguste Comte, the founder of the Positivist school, exercised no little influence over his mind in his conception of Sociology in the sixth book. In the *Autobiography* he tells us that he was long depressed by the old-world problems of Liberty and Necessity, till he found the solution in a stricter definition of what is meant by Determinism, and expounded it in his *Logic*. He also consulted various German books on Logic, though, indeed, they do not seem to have left much impress on his mind. " Here is Sterling," he says in a letter to Barclay Fox, " persuading me that I must read all manner of German logic, which, though it goes much against the grain with me, I can in no sort gainsay." He is going to give the book to his Cornish friends, but he warns them that they will find it more intelligible than interesting. He forbids them to read it through, except some chapters which he will point out. " It would be like my reading a book on mining because you live in Cornwall—it would be making friendship a burden ! " The chapters he singled out were the fifth book on Fallacies, and the chapter in the sixth book on Liberty and Necessity, " which is short, and in my judgment the

" *July*.—Common acacia, meadow-sweet, honeysuckle, sweet gale or double myrtle, Spanish broom, lime.

" In latest autumn, one stray odour, forgotten by its companions, follows at a modest distance,—the creeping clematis which adorns the cottage walls ; but the thread of continuity being broken, this solitary straggler is not included in the Calendar of Odours.

" *To* Miss CAROLINE FOX, *from her grateful friend,*

" J. S. MILL."

best in the two volumes." He is not very sanguine about the early portion of it. "I don't suppose many people will read anything so scholastic, especially as I do not profess to upset the schools, but to rebuild them, and, unluckily, everybody who cares about such subjects nowadays is of a different school from me. But that is the concern of a higher power than mine ; my concern is to bring *out* of me what is *in* me, although the world should not find, even after many days, that what is cast on the waters is wholesome bread ; nay, even although (worst of all) it may happen to be, in reality, only bread made of sawdust." Carlyle, indeed, says in his *Reminiscences* that he found Mill's talk "rather wintry and sawdustish ; " but Mill's real consciousness of what he had done came out in his remark to Miss Fox, " My family have no idea how great a man I am !"

The *System of Logic* was published, after fruitless negotiations with Murray, by Parker, in March 1843, and at once met with a great and well-deserved success. Being almost entirely a scientific work, it could not rouse the susceptibilities of those whom his recent criticism of Bentham and his partial alienation from his father had surprised and dismayed. It was in certain questions of morals and political philosophy that the suspicion had been raised that Mill was not a true Benthamite in every detail of that somewhat unlovable character. No doubt could be felt as to Mill's general position in logic, psychology, and metaphysics. Nor could such a doubt be for his contemporaries justified by the issue ; for Mill is careful to avow his acceptance of the principles of the English school—the school which, starting from Hobbes and continued in illustrious descent by such thinkers

as Locke and Hume and Hartley, held fast to experience
as their sheet-anchor, Locke's criticism of Innate Ideas
as their confession of faith, and Hartley and James
Mill's Associationism as their fighting orders. But
where Mill surpassed all that had been done heretofore
was in the clear and patient analysis of the procedure
of science, especially the careful exposition of those
great methods of experimental inquiry which fills
the larger portion of his third book. In this Mill's
only rival was Whewell, and Whewell belonged to a
different camp. No wonder, then, that Mill's *Logic*
became the text-book of the Empirical school, and was
quoted with respectful admiration by all the " Radical "
thinkers of the day. Grote, above all others, was
enthusiastic in its praise. Much as his general admiration of the author might be, as he said, "mixed with
fear," no man " conned and thumbed the book " as he
did. " John Mill's *Logic* is the best book in my library,"
were, according to Dr. Bain, his emphatic words. Bain
himself published an appreciative article on it in the
Westminster Review, more laudatory than Mill liked.
When an adverse criticism appeared in the *British Critic,*
written by Mr. W. G. Ward, Mill was by no means
displeased. Mill knew that Mr. Ward was the ally of
Newman and Pusey, and that he should be considered
worthy of so extensive a review (the article was nearly
100 pages) by thinkers who were diametrically opposed
to his tenets, gave him unbounded pleasure. " I always
hailed Puseyism," he cried, " and predicted that
Thought would sympathise with Thought, though I did
not expect to find in my own case so striking an
example."

If, however, we ask whether the *System of Logic* is destined to live as a classic on the subject, we open a question of wider issue. Clearly, it is a work which no student of the subject can possibly forego ; it has been extensively used as an instrument of education both at the Universities and elsewhere, though at Oxford, at all events, a reaction on the lines of German thought has for some time been in progress. The work is divided into six books, of which the first two, headed respectively "Names and Propositions" and "Reasoning," represent the formal aspect of Logic, and are mainly concerned with the process of Deduction. The main contention is, that the syllogism is a *petitio principii,* the conclusion being contained in the premisses, and that the real process of inference is from particular case to adjacent particular case. The second book contains Mill's attack on one of the strongholds of the *à priori* school, the belief, namely, that necessary truth is distinct in kind, and not only in degree, from contingent truth. The battle is usually fought out over the case of geometrical axioms, which Mill declares to be empirical in their origin. It is the third book, however, which is the striking feature of Mill's *Logic,* where, in twenty-five chapters, he gives an exhaustive analysis of Induction and the processes of Science. The possibility of Induction rests on the Uniformity of Nature ; but this itself is only an empirical generalisation, which merely differs from other and less trustworthy generalisations in the enormous number of observations on which it is based, and the width and variety of its scope. Laws of Nature are then explained, and we are introduced to the methods of Experimental Inquiry by which they are attained. It may be noticed in passing that we are here exchanging the narrower view of Induction as a purely logical process for the wider aspect of it as a process of scientific investigation. As a *logical* process, Induction may be defined as the inverse of Deduction, or as the mode in which we establish a general proposition: as a *scientific* process it becomes the means by which we attain to Laws of Nature. Consequently Mill holds that Logic should include the procedure of Science, which other writers on the subject had taken pains to exclude. The methods of Experimental Inquiry are four in number; the method of Agreement, the method of Difference, the method of Residues, and the method of Concomitant Variations—methods which suggest some points of comparison with the Tabulæ which Francis Bacon had detailed in the second book of his *Novum Organum*, though they form, of course, a considerable improvement on the cruder methods of the earliest of inductive logicians. Mill found considerable difficulty in getting scientific examples of purely Inductive methods, and gained much assistance in this respect from Dr. Bain, who suggested many of Liebig's theories, and (in a subsequent edition) M. Brown-Séquard's theory of cadaveric rigidity. But it was not easy to find so good an example as the famous research on Dew adduced by Herschel. As a matter of fact, most of the discoveries of Science are made by what Mill called the Deductive method—a combination of induction and deduction, or sometimes a hypothetico-deductive method. For instance, when Professor Huxley desired to show in his *Lay Sermons* that the Darwinian hypothesis is a scientific one, he explained the method which Darwin had pursued by reference to Mill's chapter on the deductive method. Purely inductive methods, as Mill had to allow, were rather of use in a Logic of Proof than a Logic of Discovery. The fourth book of Mill's *Logic*, called "Operations subsidiary to Deduction," is a general receptacle for a number of subjects which Mill did not know where to place, and Dr. Bain* suggests that it contains the materials for a Logic of Definition and Classification. The fifth and sixth books require no particular analysis for our purpose, one being concerned with a classification of Fallacies, and the other with the Logic of Moral Sciences, in which Mill made considerable use of Comte's speculations on Sociology.

If we regard the work as a whole, we are forced to distinguish its scientific character from its metaphysical groundwork. Probably no other work on Logic can give the reader so clear an idea of what Science is and what it is doing; and its merits in this respect have received emphatic testimony from scientists themselves. On the other hand, it might be urged that Logic somewhat unduly extends its boundaries when it covers all that Mill makes it cover; and especially that it ought to rest on sounder metaphysical foundations than can be discovered in the work of Mill. If it be true that these foundations include irreconcilable dogmas, then the shiftiness of the groundwork must in time make itself felt in every department of the superstructure.

We begin with the title. Mill describes his work as "The Principles of Evidence and the Methods

* Bain : *J. S. Mill*, p. 67.

6

of Scientific Investigation." Now, every writer has to formulate his own definition of Logic, and Mill is not slow to explain that he understands by Logic the Science of Proof or Evidence. If that be so, we have his position as contrasted with those who make Logic consist in an exhibition of the Formal Laws of Thought; and also with those who, like Herschel and Whewell, make Logic essentially the Science of Discovery. But if we return to the title, we are not quite sure of the last contrast. Mill very clearly enrols himself as a disciple of Material Logic, rather than of Formal; but if Logic is merely the Science of Proof, how is it also concerned (as the general title states) with Scientific Investigation? According to the stricter definition of Mill, Logic is the organon of Science; according to the looser title of his book, it is a part of Science. Perhaps this is not an important point in itself; but it becomes important when we come to the third book, the book which deals with the methods of Induction. Are these, we ask, methods of Discovery or methods of Proof? At first Mill seemed to treat them as methods of Discovery; then, in answer to a criticism of Whewell, he treats them as methods of Proof only, though the first of the methods, that of agreement, could never establish its title to this character.

It was, perhaps, an unjustifiable confidence which led us to class Mill among the Material Logicians, and not among the Formal. For if Logic be concerned with the Matter of our Thought, and not with its Form, it is not quite clear why in the earlier books we should have, amongst other topics, a system of Categories (i. 3), and an enquiry into the validity of the Major Premiss in a Syllogism (ii. 3). In this matter, the explanation is mainly historical, and only partially logical. We know that Mill was made, at an early age, to study Greek Logic and the scholastic writers on Aristotle. We know that at a subsequent period he felt it to be his task to put fresh life into some of the older logical forms, to pour the new wine of Empiricism into the old bottles of Aristotelianism. Hence his desire to substitute for the old ten Categories some Categories of his own, which were neither parts of the Logical judgment, nor due to a grammatical analysis of the sentence, but actual divisions of Nameable things. So, too, he wishes to replace the Syllogistic mode of inference by a scientific mode, and he labours to prove that the conclusion does not *depend* on the major premiss (in which case it would be proved *by* it), but is only proved *in accordance* with it, the major premiss being a register, memorandum, or shorthand note of experience up to a given date. The whole controversy about the *petitio principii* involved in the Syllogism is a curious instance of the confusion caused by mixing up two different views of Logic. The Syllogism is an important, or rather, an archetypal process of thought, viewed in its formal aspect; for Concept, Judgment, and Syllogism represent the initial grades into which thought can be analysed. If we are not concerned with this point of view, if we are only going to regard thought as the mere correspondence of our apprehension with fact, then the Logic which is to be a Logic of Evidence should not concern itself with the formal validity of the Syllogism at all.

The peculiar weakness of Mill's theory of inference,

viz., that it proceeds from particular instance to particular instance without deducing from an universal proposition, becomes manifest in his treatment of the question of the Uniformity of Nature. For in our belief in the Uniformity of Nature we have an universal truth, which does, as a matter of fact, serve as major premiss in all our reasoning about Nature's operations. Indeed, Induction itself is dependent on the truth of this major premiss, or principle. For how are we to argue that what has held good in a set of instances already observed will also hold good in another set of instances resembling the former, except on the supposition that Nature is uniform? Mill himself admits that Induction depends on the Uniformity of Nature, and yet is forced, by his general theory of inference, to prove that Induction must somehow prove the Uniformity of Nature. We need not follow him through all the twists and windings of the attempted justification of so strange a position ; it will be enough to point out that the question practically reduces itself to the following dilemma :—Either the possibility of Induction rests upon the Uniformity of Nature, in which case our process of inference is clearly from a general or universal truth down to its particular exemplifications, or else we can only argue from particular instance to particular instance ; and in that case our belief in Nature's uniformity is strictly limited to our experience ; it becomes a merely empirical generalisation, and as such is apparently (*Logic* iii., xvi.) inferior in validity to " Laws of Nature." It is not possible for Mill to escape this dilemma by the device which recommends itself to his successors—to Mr. Herbert Spencer, for instance, and to the philosophic believers in Evolution. For with them the experience which is to prove these and similar truths is the accumulated experience of the human race through all the ages of its development, from which our own and limited individual experience can take its start as an assured and incontrovertible body of truths. But Mill's " experience " is not like Mr. Herbert Spencer's ; it is not " race-experience," but " individual-experience." He is, therefore, always open to the charge of trying to get wide-reaching truths out of the changing and fragmentary experiences of our three-score years and ten. The solution is paradoxically inadequate to the problem.

Mill's metaphysical system may be described as transitional, and we can now more precisely indicate the principles between which he oscillates. He comes half-way between Hume and Herbert Spencer in certain doctrines, while in others he apparently tries to mediate between the school of Descartes and the school of Locke. To Hume all truth depended on individual experiences ; to Herbert Spencer some truths are *à priori* to the individual, but *à posteriori* to the race. In Mill's case we have (to refer back to the example we have been just considering) the desire to make Induction rest as a process on some large principle which individual experience could never substantiate, while all the time his professed belief is that, apart from individual experience, there can be no origin for truth. So, too, with some of the theories which are expounded at the end of the second book of the *Logic* and the beginning of the third. One of these is the nature of geometrical axioms as a part of so-called necessary truth. Mill's desire is to explode the *à priori* view which the Cartesian school held of the origin of knowledge. There can not be for

Mill, any more than for Locke, *à priori* or innate principles. Consequently, geometrical axioms are said to be experimental. But the elements with which they deal are for Mill not experimental, but ideal. They deal with straight lines and perfect circles. Lines perfectly straight, and circles perfectly round are not found in actual experience, but are ideal. Hence Mill takes up the curious position that though experience alone *proves* that two straight lines can not enclose a space, yet experience can not seemingly *present* us with lines perfectly straight. As, however, unless the lines are perfectly straight, two of them might enclose a space, we are only confused by this apparent attempt to combine two opposite points of view, the idealistic and the experimental. The same oscillation, the same desire to combine antagonistic positions, meet us in Mill's discussion of the relation between Cause and Effect. The idealistic school—the school which descended from Descartes—laid stress on the invariable and unconditional character of the relation between Cause and Effect as a proof that it was mental, *à priori*, and therefore not derived from Experience. Mill, in accordance with his general acceptance of the doctrines of Locke and Hume, thinks that the relation of Cause and Effect is purely experimental, depending on an observed series of experiences. Yet he goes on to assert that this experimental relation can and must be invariable and unconditional. But how can experience give rise to an invariable and unconditional relation? Even Mill himself, despite his definitions, can not admit such a possibility. For so clearly is our notion of Cause and Effect derived from our experience that we are, he thinks, forced to admit that in distant parts of the stellar regions, where our experience has not penetrated, events may follow without being caused. What, then, becomes of the invariable and unconditional sequence of Effect on Cause? We might go on multiplying instances of the same oscillation between different theories. It will perhaps, however, be better to connect this peculiarity in Mill's logical position with a view which seems to have taken even stronger hold of him in later years. So receptive was he of other men's views, so much did he—after his own experiences in his mental crisis—dislike dogmatic and intolerant statements, that it was a favourite belief of his that the truth lay somewhere between two opposite theories. This comes out very strongly in his *Liberty*, written some years after his *Logic*. One of the reasons why all opinions should be published in perfect freedom from legal restraint is just this doctrine about Truth, as being placed half-way between two opposites. Another reason is connected with his Individualism. All progress, all variety, depend on individual efforts. Just as thought can not progress unless different individuals in different spheres are allowed to bring their quota to the general store, so, too, national welfare is held by Mill in his *Political Economy* to depend on the principle of *laisser faire*, untrammelled by positive legislation. And this point, too, connects itself with his *Logic*. For individual effort is naturally enough the source of all welfare, if individual experience is actually the source of all our knowledge. Thus Individualism involves Liberty of Dissent, and Liberty of Dissent is justified by the assumption that Truth, in the majority of cases, forms a sort of boundary line between opposing factions.

Whether such a doctrine is to be accepted or not, it is obvious enough that it acts disastrously on the clearness and consistency of philosophical doctrines. Receptivity of mind is valuable only so far as in exposition it is balanced by certain fixed and unalterable points of view. But if the expounder of a system of Logic is at the same time always absorbing theories, even from his enemies, we may admire his character, but we cannot always understand his position. Let us take one final instance from the sixth book of the *Logic*. In writing on Sociology Mill is very much under the influence of Auguste Comte and Positivism. He takes from him his general conception of the Science, and, to a large extent, his views on its method. But in Comte Sociology was deduced directly from Biology: from the physical organism we are to advance to the social organism. A consequence is that Psychology as an introspective science is by Comte discarded, and Cerebral Physiology is put in its place. This Mill will by no means admit. He belongs to a school of English psychologists, and he cannot set his seal to the incompetence of his teachers. Psychology, in consequence, must be made the foundation of Sociology. The discovery is then made that there is yet a link missing. We cannot at once advance from the laws of mind to the laws which govern society. We must introduce a science which shall deal with the laws of character, the science which Mill terms Ethology. Without Ethology he maintains Sociology to be impossible. But can there be a science of Character? Mill, at all events, has to give it up. For some time after the *Logic* came out he was busy with an attempt to sketch such a science. But he had to confess his failure, and his failure with Ethology fatally interfered with the larger project, which he entertained, of executing a work on Sociology. That he despaired of making anything out of Ethology is proved, acccording to Dr. Bain, by his betaking himself to the composition of his *Political Economy.**

* Bain : *J. S. Mill.* p. 79.

CHAPTER V.

RICARDO'S DISCIPLE—(1843-1849).

THE publication of the *Logic* brought no relaxation of activity to Mill. We are now in the period of his life which marks the highest tide, not, indeed, of his industry, which was always continuous and excessive, but of that literary achievement by which a man secures his place in the history of his country. One great claim to remembrance he had already put forth in 1843 : he was now preparing his second great contribution to the best thought of the age—the *Political Economy*, which was published in 1848. The intervening years were not wholly occupied with this project. In 1842 he wrote a masterly review of Bailey's Theory of Vision in the *Westminster Review*, which contained a vindication of Berkeley's metaphysical essay on Sight as against the strictures of his critic. In the same year he seems to have had a slight attack of illness, perhaps in consequence of his severe loss in the American Repudiation, and was unable to take his usual walk home from the India House to Kensington Square; but on October 3rd he writes, "I am quite well and strong, and now walk the whole way to and from Kensington without the self-indulgence of *omnibi*." In 1843, besides the publication of his *Logic*, he wrote an article on "Michelet" for the *Edinburgh Review*, which he forecasts "will make some of its readers stare." It contained a defence of the papacy and the celibacy of the clergy, argued on philosophical grounds, as a means of preserving the world from barbarism; but it does not seem to have produced the consequences which Mill anticipated. The article came out in 1844, and was followed by "The Claims of Labour" and "Guizot," both contributed to the *Edinburgh Review* in the succeeding year. Then, in 1846, there was a labour of love in the review of the first two volumes of Grote's *Greek History* in the same periodical; while, in 1847, he wrote articles on Irish affairs in the *Chronicle*. It is one evidence of the thoroughness with which this occasional writing was performed, that he read through the whole of the *Iliad* and *Odyssey* in the original before his article on Grote's *History*. It illustrates, also, Mill's dislike of the idea of any generic difference between men and women that he prevailed upon Grote to alter, in a second edition, the words "masculine" and "feminine," which the historian had applied to the difference between the scientific and artistic activity of the Greeks.* His articles in the *Morning Chronicle* were principally devoted to an urgent recommendation to reclaim the waste lands in Ireland, and convert them into peasant proprietorships—a topic appearing again in the *Political Economy*, which was, perhaps, suggested to his mind by his friend, Mr. Thornton.

Perhaps, however, the most important incident in these

* Bain : *J. S. Mill*, p. 86.

years was his friendship and correspondence with the French Positivist philosopher, Auguste Comte. " Have you ever looked into Comte's *Cours de Philosophie Positive ?* " he writes to Dr. Bain on October 15, 1841. " He makes some mistakes, but, on the whole, I think it very near the grandest work of this age." His correspondence with Comte began in 1841 and lasted to 1846. The greatest warmth of feeling between the two is shown in the letters of 1842 and 1843. After that it somewhat cools, though as late as 1846, when Comte had lost his Clotilde, he received an affectionate letter of condolence from Mill. But it was impossible for a man of the high and generous feeling which Mill so uniformly displayed to be on intimate terms with one who was so utterly different to himself both in tone of character and habitual range of thoughts. Comte, more perhaps than any other philosopher, except Francis Bacon, demands from his critics a clear severance between the character of his life and the character of his intellect. One of the most comprehensive and synthetic thinkers of his age was, in domestic affairs, perhaps one of the meanest and smallest. When he was turned out from the position of Examiner at the Polytechnic School at Paris, he did not scruple to demand subsidies from his friends, nor to revile them if they refused to contribute. Mill, who, despite his losses through the American Repudiation, had been forward in offers of pecuniary help, first found a topic of disagreement in the position of women ; and then had finally to convey to Comte that Grote and Molesworth, whom he had interested in the case of the disappointed Examiner, were disinclined to give any further assistance. Comte, who in his correspondence shows much of the airs of a literary *parvenu* of course, could not understand such a refusal, and wrote to Mill a long lecture on the relations between rich men and philosophers. Grote was, however, obdurate, having conceived a strong dislike to Comte's sociological theories; indeed, it became almost impossible for Mill to continue the correspondence with a writer so wanting in ordinary taste. A final letter was written on the occasion of the death of Comte's Clotilde. Perhaps Mill was glad to be able to finish the correspondence with a subject in which there was no opportunity for controversy or angry retort.

The Principles of Political Economy was published, as we have already seen, in the beginning of 1848. Many circumstances made its publication a notable event amidst the higher circles of the literary world. Mill had been known to be a student of the subject since his earlier years. In boyish walks with his father economic topics had been discussed, and it was principally owing to these conversations that James Mill's *Elements of Political Economy* was produced. Moreover, the friendship between the elder Mill and Ricardo was notorious, as was also the fact that, had it not been for his friend's solicitations, Ricardo's theories would never have seen the light of day. John Mill himself had made some preliminary contributions to the subject, which he had written as early as 1830 and 1831, but which had only been published in 1844, under the title of *Essays on Unsettled Questions in Political Economy*. The first of these dealt with the laws of interchange between nations, and was sufficient to prove how close a study he had made of Ricardo's theory of foreign exchanges. The second and third dealt respectively with the

influence of consumption on production, and the meaning of the words "productive" and "unproductive,"
as applied to labour, consumption, and expenditure.
The fourth showed still more decisively the influence of
Ricardo, as it was concerned with the justification of
the theorem, that "profits depend on wages, rising as
wages fall, and falling as wages rise." The fifth essay
was on the method of political economy, a subject
treated also in the subsequent work, which forms a
point of some importance in the estimation of Mill's
position. There was, besides these definite contributions on Mill's part to the literature of the subject,
a general expectation that the differences and dis-
crepancies between political economists would shortly
disappear, and that Mill's exposition would be the great
instrument in settling the essential principles. Colonel
Torrens declared that in twenty years there would not
exist a doubt respecting any of its more fundamental
principles. Professor Sidgwick points out the reason for
this confidence. "The prosperity," he says, "that
followed on the abolition of the corn-laws gave practical
men a most impressive and satisfying proof of the
soundness of the abstract reasoning by which the
expediency of free trade had been inferred." It was, in
consequence, generally believed that 'the state of
polemical discussion' was passed, and that a really
constructive era had dawned.

We, who live with forty years' additional experience of
the changing fortunes of political economy, know how
little these sanguine expectations were destined to be
realised. Much has been changed in the interval; to
some extent we have gone back to older views; in some

respects we are still looking for that wider synthesis which is to make the unsettled questions fall into their proper place.   But the value of Mill's work can only be understood in reference to what came before him as well as to the speculations which succeeded him, and it becomes necessary, however briefly, to trace the development of economical thought in England.   For our purposes, we need go no further back than that mercantile system which forms the first phase of the modern thought on the subject.   The general position of the mercantilists can be sketched somewhat as follows.   They thought that money and wealth were identical, and that a country, therefore, was bound to attract to itself the greatest share of the precious metals.   Each country, they argued, must export as much as it can, and import as little as it can, receiving the difference of the two values in gold and silver—a difference which was called " the balance of trade."   In order to secure such a balance, Governments must either prohibit, or put high duties on, the importation of foreign wares ; they must resort also to bounties on the export of home manufactures, and restrictions on the export of the precious metals, in pursuit of the same object.   It is not difficult to understand where the mistakes of such a theory lay.   It is obvious that the mercantilists overestimated the importance of possessing a large amount of the precious metals ; and the newer ideas, which were promulgated by Petty and North, about 1691, were concerned with showing that national wealth depended rather on the gifts of nature and the labour of man.   Further, it is clear that foreign trade should not be so unduly estimated in relation to domestic. nor should the industry which works up materials be considered so superior to that which produces them. "The balance of trade" is a fiction, the real aim for the economist being the attempt to secure for the whole population the necessaries and conveniences of life. Finally, such devices as prohibitions, protective duties, bounties, and monopolies, ought to be discarded as being in reality impediments to trade, which only requires as its indispensable condition the freedom of industry.

The second phase of modern economic thought may, perhaps, be said to begin with the "physiocrats" (Quesnay, Gournay, and Dupont de Nemours), who, amongst many errors, brought into prominence principles which were destined to play a considerable part in subsequent speculations. The physiocratic theory begins with the idea of a *Jus Naturæ*, a simple, impressive, and beneficial code established by Nature herself. From this conception flowed such principles as the belief that all individuals have the same natural rights, and that Government is a necessary evil. In relation to trade, then, the ideal motto of Governments should be *laissez-faire, laissez-passer*,—the highest point of negative indifference, in order that labour might be completely unfettered and undisturbed. Immensely more valuable as is the work of Adam Smith, it yet proceeds on much the same lines. It is true that the conception of a code of Nature is put into the background, but the belief in the individual, with his desire for gain and the necessity for his freedom, is the animating spirit of the *Wealth of Nations*. Where Adam Smith is honourably distinguished from his predecessors, and even from some of his successors, lies in his copious illustrations of tenets by actual experience, and his continuous references to historical data in support of his theories. Yet, what the German critics, Roscher and Hildebrand, derisively call "Smithianismus" has defects which have recently become patent to modern eyes. If Smith's conception of the social economy is essentially individualistic, it must further be added that the "economic man," on whom the whole system turns, is a hypothetical being from whom all motives, other than the selfish and the interested, have been carefully abstracted. It results that the economic advantage of society must be held to be identical with the economic advantage of the individual, and that the system of Smith becomes too absolute in character because its regard is exclusively directed to man as an abstract being rather than to man as he has been made by the discipline of history and the courses of civilisation. But whatever be the merits or demerits of Adam Smith, it is certain that the whole tendency of his successor, Ricardo, is to exaggerate the characteristic points, and to leave out that saving reference to actual experience which formed the strong point of his predecessor. Ricardo, at all events, moves in a world of abstractions; the "economic man," actuated by a single principle of greed, stalks everywhere through his pages; nor has custom, apparently, any chance against competition in industry; nor is combination regarded as a possible expedient in solving the problems of labour. The famous doctrine of Rent is only hypothetically true in the most advanced industrial communities, however much the implied theory that the interests of landlords are permanently in opposition to

7

those of other classes may have suited the democratic character of current Benthamism. Comte, indeed, remarks in one of his letters to Mill,* that Benthamism was a derivative from political economy and from the system of natural liberty, and the truth of the remark is seen in the attitude of men like McCulloch, James Mill, and others, to the Ricardian principles. Further weak points in Ricardo himself were his habitual assumptions that capital could be so easily transferred from one undertaking to another, that labour could also be so easily transferred from one industry to another,† and that both capitalists and labourers might be expected to know all about the prospects of industry, not only in their own, but in other countries. To these must be added, as still further demerits, Ricardo's extreme looseness of phraseology,‡ and the want of any explanation of the appropriate method by which political economy should be studied.

We have called Mill Ricardo's disciple, but it must not be supposed that he was in any sense a servile follower of his master. He clearly held it his mission to justify Ricardo to the world, and he speaks of Ricardo's "superior lights" in comparison with his predecessors. But his design was much larger than a mere illustration of Ricardian principles. The object of his book, as he

---

* *Lettres d'A. Comte à J. S. Mill*, p. 4.

† Adam Smith knew better. "It appears, evidently from experience, that man is, of all sorts of luggage, the most difficult to be transported."—*Wealth of Nations*, Book I., c. viii.

‡ Senior called him "the most incorrect writer who ever attained philosophical eminence." Quoted by Ingram.—*History of Political Economy*, p. 123.

himself tells us, was to exhibit economic phenomena in relation to the most advanced conceptions of his own time on the general philosophy of society—to do, in fact, for the nineteenth century what Adam Smith had done for the eighteenth. In pursuance of this aim there were many points in his treatise which were not only valuable in themselves, but exhibited a distinct advance on anything which had gone before them. He himself used to say that Ricardo had supplied the backbone of the science, but, as Cairnes remarked in a notice of Mill's labours in the *Examiner*, it is not less certain that the limbs, the joints, and the muscular developments were the work of Mill. We may take, for example, the development which Mill gives of Ricardo's doctrine of foreign trade, where the skeleton is clothed with flesh, and principles of the most abstract kind are translated into concrete language, and brought to explain familiar facts. Or we may look at Mill's doctrine of the economic nature of land, which, though it has been sometimes denied, is clearly, in its views of the peculiar nature of landed property and its doctrines of "the unearned increment," a direct deduction from Ricardo's theory of Rent. More originality is shown by Mill in the introduction of new premisses, which very often largely alter the deductions to be drawn from old principles. For instance, in reference to the effect which the growth of society has on the minimum point of wages, Mill remarks that this minimum is not a *physical* but a *moral* minimum, and is, therefore, capable of being altered with the changes of character in the population at large. Hence, instead of a weary pessimism as to the future condition of the labourer, we have the suggested chance of improvement as his moral character improves ; and the chapter, "the Future of the Industrial Classes," is very different in tone and speculation from anything we find in Ricardo. So, too, Mill sees readily enough how much the influence of custom serves to modify the stress of competition, and how clearly the real regulator of rent over the greater part of the habitable globe is not competition only, but competition, custom, and the absolute will of the owner of the soil. " This recognition," says Cairnes, " threw an entirely new light over the whole problem of land-tenure, and plainly furnished grounds for legislative interference in the contracts between landlords and tenants. Its application to Ireland was obvious, and Mill himself did not hesitate to urge the application with all the energy and enthusiasm which he invariably threw into every cause that he espoused." On another point Mill also departed from Ricardo. In deference to the arguments of his friend, Mr. Thornton, he finally gave up the "wage-fund" theory, and though here Cairnes thinks him wrong, there are many modern economists who believe that his newer position was entirely in the right. Both Mill and Cairnes, however, are agreed in one important modification of previous doctrine. By both of these writers it is maintained that economic art, or the application of principles to practice, does not follow straight from economic science. Application to practice demands other considerations than those purely economical—a point the importance of which will come out in the sequel.

In the discussion of Mill's *Logic* in the last chapter, it was suggested that Mill represented a transitional

state of opinion, between Hume and Herbert Spencer
on the one hand, and the school of empiricism and
idealism on the other. In this position was found
the explanation of many of the inconsistencies which
analysis seemed to reveal in the fundamental dogmas
of the work. Up to 1843, in point of fact, the tide
in Mill's mind seemed to be strongly setting in the
direction of a reform of Benthamism by means of
Coleridge, Carlyle, and the Germans, owing especially to
the influence of John Sterling. Somewhere about that
period it received a check ; and the check was due to
Comte, the Socialists, and, perhaps in a lesser degree,
Mrs. Taylor. We have now to ask the same question
with regard to the *Political Economy.* The system
which Mill inherited, and in which he was trained,
was clearly the doctrine of Ricardo and Malthus. Were
there any fresh influences acting on him, and if so, was
their character consistent with the earlier views?

One of the earliest critics of the system of Ricardo
was a professor at Haileybury, Richard Jones, who lived
between the years 1790-1855, and whose *Essay on the
Distribution of Wealth, and on the Sources of Taxation,*
was published in 1831, seventeen years before the work
of Mill. Jones was dissatisfied at once with the method
and the results of Ricardo's theories. "If," he said,
"we wish to make ourselves acquainted with the
economy and arrangements by which the different
nations of the earth produce and distribute their
revenues, I really know but of one way to attain our
object, and that is, to look and see. We must get
comprehensive views of facts, that we may arrive at
principles that are truly comprehensive. If we take a

different method, if we snatch at general principles, and
content ourselves with confined observations, two things
will happen to us.   First, what we call general principles
will often be found to have no generality—we shall set
out with declaring propositions to be universally true,
which at every step of our further progress we shall be
obliged to confess are frequently false; and, secondly,
we shall miss a great mass of useful knowledge which
those who advance to principles by a comprehensive
examination of facts necessarily meet with on their
road."* It is clear that we here meet with something like a revolt against the *à priori*, deductive
method of Ricardo.   Nor was Jones inclined to admit
some of Ricardo's conclusions.   He animadverts on
the theory of Rent, and declares that besides competition, which, under the supposed conditions, might
affect " farmers' rents," there was also custom, which
indubitably affected " peasant-rents."   Here was much
the same modification which Mill afterwards brought
forward.   He further made a classification of peasant-
rents into serf, metayer, ryot, and cottier, and the
classification reappears in substance in the pages of
Mill.   In other points of his criticism—such as the
denial that the interests of landlords are necessarily
opposed to those of other classes, and that wages can
rise only at the expense of profits—Mill was not at one
with him ; but it is perhaps true, as Mr. Ingram
remarks, that Mill, while using Jones' work, gave his
merits but faint recognition.

The *Philosophie Positive* of Comte—at least the two
first volumes—was brought over to England in 1837

* Quoted by Ingram in his *History of Political Economy*, p. 143.

by Wheatstone, who always claimed the merit of its
introduction. Mill read them about the end of 1837, or
beginning of 1838, and was profoundly struck with them.
The effect was seen in the sixth book of his *Logic*, as has
been already remarked. Now, while Comte thought but
meanly of Political Economy as it was pursued in England, he sketched out a great science of Social Physics,
which he believed was destined to include speculations
on economical subjects in a larger framework. With his
criticisms of English political economy, Mill, of course,
could not agree, and stigmatised them as essentially
shallow and superficial. But the new science of Sociology
made such an impression on him that for some time he
busied himself with the attempt to write a large book on
the same subject. In reality, however, Comte's scheme
involved principles which were fundamentally different
from his own. Comte believed that Sociology was
one science which should be studied in its totality,
because all social phenomena had a certain solidarity
—an idea which made a separate economic science an
impossibility. Its method, moreover, was not to be
deductive, but to be based on a systematic historical
comparison, while the historical spirit was conspicuously
absent in the *doctrinaires* of the eighteenth century.
Inasmuch as it was to be studied historically, the science
demanded a division between a statical theory of society
(the influences acting on a given state at any one time),
and a dynamical theory (the steps by which a historical
state was evolved out of preceding states). This distinction was eagerly seized on by Mill, though perhaps
he never saw how it reacted on his older views of an
abstract treatment of economics, and how it necessitated

the substitution for them of a doctrine of the laws of the economic development of nations. He does, indeed, attempt in Book IV. of his work, a treatment of Economic Dynamics, but his critics do not appear to regard this portion as one of the most successful.

There were other influences also in the air, besides the influence of the *Philosophie Positive.* Chief among these was the theory of the Socialists, the work of men like St. Simon, Fourier, Proudhon, and Lassalle. Two ideas at least were here prominent: on the one hand, the destruction of the negative theory of Government; on the other, the limitation of the individualistic greed for wealth and dislike of labour. There was, besides, the German school of economists, men like Wilhelm Roscher, whose work appeared in 1843, and Bruno Hildebrand, whose first volume appeared in 1848. In them a prominent view was the necessity of accentuating the moral elements in economic study, and putting the selfish into the background. Even in England the spirit of change was abroad in the writings of Carlyle, with his professed antagonism to the tenets of the Manchester school.

If we look at Mill as being in the midst of, if not affected by, such influences as these, we shall understand the reason for some of those doubts which are suggested to some minds by his work. The way in which he turns to Political Economy is in itself significant. It will be remembered that, after the publication of his *Logic,* his thoughts were for some time occupied with Sociology, and that he abandoned the subject because, in the way in which he interpreted the science, it was necessarily dependent on Ethology, and of Ethology he failed to make any real scheme. It was then that he betook himself to Political Economy. The consequence was that the relation in which his newer subject stood to Sociology was never perspicuously explained. Was Political Economy a part of the larger science, or was it only a sort of preparatory study? If we look at the title of his larger work, *Principles of Political Economy, with some of their Applications to Social Philosophy,* the doubt is suggested whether Political Economy is in reality such an integral portion of Sociology that its separate study cannot be otherwise than abstract and hypothetical. But elsewhere he speaks of it as " carved out of the general body of the science of society," a sentence which clearly affirms its necessary subordination. The reason of such hesitation, if it be hesitation, is, probably, that he had his own version of what the science of society meant, and that his version did not in every respect correspond to that of Comte, from whom, nevertheless, he derived it. To Comte, Social Physics were to be studied historically. This was one consequence of the distinction he drew between Social Statics and Social Dynamics. This, too, was the result of his general assumption that as we rise in the series of sciences from simplicity to complexity of data, the general inductive methods are to be aided by special devices. Thus Biology demands the use of the comparative method, and Social Physics, in its turn, because of the increased complexity of its data, demands the use of the historical method. But to Mill, Sociology was dependent on Ethology, the science of human character, and it in its turn was dependent on Psychology, the science of the general laws of mind.

Sociology was, therefore, to be studied deductively in great measure, because of this intimate dependence on the sciences of mind. It is true that it must also be studied by the inverse deductive method (which is Mill's name for the historical method), and so far as this reservation went, it became a science apart. But Political Economy, at all events, might, whatever its relations to Sociology, be studied deductively, as dependent on the laws of human nature; and thus Mill could still keep himself in alliance with the views of Ricardo. In the fifth of his *Essays on Unsettled Questions* he declares with some dogmatism that the *à priori* method is the only one which is applicable, and that the *à posteriori* method "is altogether inefficacious in those sciences (the social) as a means of arriving at any considerable body of valuable truth." But then came in the later work the reminiscence of Comte's distinction between the Statics and Dynamics of Society, which he in many parts of his book values so highly. He therefore tries to save himself by a distinction between two sorts of economic inquiry, only one of which could be treated by the *à posteriori* method. The chief merit of his treatise, he says, lies in its distinction between the theory of Production and the theory of Distribution. Production is based on unalterable natural laws, which could therefore only be studied *à priori*; while the principles of Distribution, which are modified by successive changes in society, could only be gathered *à posteriori*. Yet even here he is not consistent. For in the treatment of Production, as Mr. Sidgwick has pointed out, he proceeds by analysing our common empirical knowledge of the facts of industry, and this, if it is not formally induction, is clearly a sort of induction. The pressure of the old Ricardian theory on his mind is thus struggling with the newer lights derived from Comte.

Other ambiguities are not difficult of detection, especially in relation to Malthusian views and the theories of the Socialists. It is not easy to be sure of Mill's attitude towards Malthus. On the whole he seems to accept his doctrine, and to incorporate it with the deductions from Ricardo's theory of rent. He adds, indeed, an idea which is not found in Malthus. "Malthus himself and some of his followers, such as Thomas Chalmers, regarded late marriages as the proper means of restricting numbers ; an extension to the lower classes of the same prudence that maintains the position of the upper and middle classes. Mill prescribes a further pitch of self-denial, the continence of married couples. At least such is the more obvious interpretation to be put upon his language. It was the opinion of many, that while his estimate of pure sentimental affection was more than enough, his estimate of the sexual passion was too low."* It is clear, at all events, that he believed in the necessity of restricting the population. Yet it might perhaps be maintained that such moral restraints are dependent for their working on the individual responsibility for the support of a family ; and this idea might be difficult to preserve in the Socialistic theories to which in many parts of his work he gives such weight. For, especially in the third edition of his *Political Economy* (after the French Revolution of 1848), he tells us that, though still believing in individual liberty of action, he

* Bain : *J. S. Mill*, p. 89.

turned his thoughts to "a common ownership in the raw material of the globe, and an equal participation in all the benefits of combined labour." Tempted thus by Socialist schemes, he yet will not give himself up to them. To improve the existing distribution of wealth he looks hopefully in the direction of the Socialistic writers; but though thus expecting the dawn of a newer order, he will in the meantime be content with the old views of private interest.*

"His was not a historical head," says Roscher of Mill, and thus, though he surveys "the promised land," he yet will die on some Ricardian Pisgah. Promised land, indeed, the newer political economy may never furnish. But amongst the wildernesses in which the students of the science still seem to be wandering, there is one beacon. The idea, which is of indubitable value in the German historical school, is the necessity of accentuating the moral element in economic study. We have seen that both Mill and Cairnes desire to keep separate economic science and economic art, possibly owing to the conviction that if the principles of economic science, with its assumptions of individual greed and selfishness, were immediately applied to practice, the results would be, if not immoral, at least non-moral. But if we ask, how the step can be taken from theory to practice, in what way the abstract laws can be translated into concrete facts, the answer in economy, as well as in other departments, can only be furnished by morals. Morals, in fact, form the stepping-stone between principle and

* Cf. "The Chapters on Socialism" contributed (posthumously) to the *Fortnightly Review* in 1879.

act, and thus the necessity which the German economists feel is amply justified. For surely the uses
of wealth are at least as important as the modes
in which it can be acquired, and have an enormous effect on the moral condition of a people.
Whatever else may or may not be required from the
economics of the future—whether the tendency may be
to emphasise the functions of government, or whether
the pendulum may swing back again, as Mr. Herbert
Spencer desires, to the doctrine of *laisser-faire*—no
theory can be held to meet the problems of our age,
unless it aids in the formation, both in the higher and
lower regions of the industrial world, of profound convictions as to social duties. The theory of individual
rights has had its day : that of duty must take its place.*

* Cf. an interesting chapter on the Future in Mr. Ingram's
History of Political Economy, from which much has been taken in
the views indicated above. Roscher's works referred to are—
*Grundriss zu Vorlesungen über die Staatswirthschaft nach gesch-
ichtlicher Methode*, and *Zur Geschichte der Englischen Volkswirth-
schaftslehre*. Cf., too, Jevons's *Future of Political Economy.—
Fortnightly Review*, 1876.

CHAPTER VI.

MRS. TAYLOR—(1848-1858).

FROM the two great literary labours of Mill, the *Logic* and the *Political Economy*, we turn to some of the incidents of his domestic life. There is possibly a comparative failure of energy after 1848, due to the enormous strain of the two winters' work in 1842-3 and 1846-7. One instance is quoted by Dr. Bain. After the appearance of Ferrier's *Institutes*—a metaphysical work on the lines of what is known as subjective Idealism—Mill said that he could have dashed off an article much as he did on the publication of Bailey's Theory of Vision. But no article was forthcoming, and his papers in the *Westminster Review* seem not to have been so frequent as of yore. One cause of this was undoubtedly ill-health. In the summer of 1848 he had a bad fall in Kensington Gardens, which was followed by an affection of the eyes. "Lame and unable to use his eyes," says Dr. Bain, "I never saw him in such a state of despair." Six years later he had the illness to which he makes allusion in the *Autobiography*. An attack on the chest, ending in the partial destruction of one lung, he did his best to cure by an eight months' absence from England, during which he visited Italy, Sicily, and Greece. According to Sir James Clark, the local disease was not so serious as the general debility, which, in the opinion of his medical adviser, would probably prevent him from doing any other considerable work. Peacock, who was the head of his office in the India House, told Grote that his absence was much felt, and it was no doubt a considerable relief, not only to his friends, but to his official chief, when he returned to London with his health tolerably re-established. The literary work of this period does not seem to have been great. He published in the *Westminster Review*, in 1849, a vindication of the French Revolution of the preceding year, in answer to the strictures of his father's friend, Lord Brougham. This was followed three years later by an article on Whewell's *Elements of Morality*, equalling in the savageness of its attack his previous diatribe against Professor Sedgwick. Then came a final paper on Grote's *History of Greece*, which he published in the *Edinburgh Review*. His official duties became heavy when, in 1857, the East India Company was threatened with extinction. He had become head of the office, owing to the retirement of Peacock in 1856, and it fell to his lot to draft a petition to Parliament on behalf of his employers. This petition was pronounced by Earl Grey to be the ablest State-paper he had ever read. Despite his earnest protest, however, the Bill passed for the transfer of the Indian Government to the Crown, and Mill retired from official work. He was applied to by Lord Stanley to serve on the new Indian Council, but he declined the offer on the plea of failing health.

The whole of this period is, so far as Mill's domestic

life is concerned, overshadowed by Mrs. Taylor. Introduced to her as early as 1831, at a dinner party at Mr.
Taylor's house, where were present Roebuck, W. J. Fox,
and Harriet Martineau, the acquaintance rapidly ripened
into intimacy, and the intimacy into a friendship, which
Mill himself was never weary of describing in terms that
could not but appear extravagant to others. In some of the
presentation copies of his *Political Economy* he wrote the
following dedication :—" To Mrs. John Taylor, who of all
persons known to the author is the most highly qualified
either to originate or to appreciate speculation on social
advancement, this work is, with the highest respect and
esteem, dedicated." An article on " the Enfranchisement of Women" was made the occasion for another
panegyric. The dedication of Mill's work on *Liberty*
is well known.* Finally, the pages of the Autobiography
ring with the dithyrambic praise of " his almost
infallible counsellor." There is a touch of fatuousness
in all this, which can be accounted for only on the

---

* " To the beloved and deplored memory of her who was the
inspirer, and in part the author, of all that is best in my writings—
the friend and wife, whose exalted sense of truth and right was my
strongest incitement, and whose approbation was my chief reward—
I dedicate this volume. Like all that I have written for many
years, it belongs as much to her as to me ; but the work as it
stands has had, in a very insufficient degree, the inestimable
advantage of her revision ; some of the most important portions
having been reserved for a more careful re-examination, which they
are now never destined to receive. Were I but capable of interpreting to the world one half the great thoughts and noble
feelings which are buried in her grave, I should be the medium of
a greater benefit to it, than is ever likely to arise from anything that
I can write, unprompted and unassisted by her all but unrivalled
wisdom."

principle that every man carries a dead poet within his breast. Mill had, indeed, tried to write verse, at his father's orders, in the immaturity of his powers, but the companionship with Mrs. Taylor was the poem of his lifetime. Meanwhile Egeria cast an apple of discord among his friends. His father taxed him with being in love with another man's wife; his acquaintance did not dare to mention her name; while those who were less cautious suffered the penalty of their temerity. Amongst others, Roebuck, Mrs. Grote, Mrs. Austin, Miss Harriet Martineau, and perhaps Lady Harriet Baring, owed their dismissal to allusions to the forbidden subject. The husband accepted the situation with all the discomfort it entailed, and Mrs. Taylor lived with her daughter in a lodging in the country, until, in 1851, Mill, after the death of her husband, made her his wife. It seems that no one was asked to call on her. Grote would have liked to do so, yet did not dare ; but an utter estrangement from both mother and sister was one of the first consequences of the union. Opinions differed as to her merits. George Mill, one of Mill's younger brothers, said that she was "a clever and remarkable woman, but nothing like what John took her to be." Carlyle, in his *Reminiscences*, utters enigmatic sentences about her. She was "vivid," or "iridescent;" she was "pale and passionate and sad-looking, a living-romance heroine of the royallest volition and questionable destiny"—epithets which might have been intended to be complimentary, but were certainly ambiguous. Mrs. Carlyle wrote that she might be her friend, but she is deemed dangerous. Carlyle adds, that she was worse than dangerous—she was patronising. On one occasion

Mill and his wife were brought into close contact with the Carlyles. The MS. of the first volume of the *French Revolution* was lent to Mill, and was accidentally burnt by Mrs. Mill's servant. Mill and his wife drove up to Carlyle's door—Mrs. Mill speechless, Mill so full of of conversation that he detained Carlyle with desperate attempts at loquacity for two hours. He made, however, a substantial reparation by prevailing on his victim to accept half of the two hundred pounds which he offered.* Mrs. Taylor died in 1858, after seven years of happy companionship with Mill, and was buried at Avignon. The inscription which Mill wrote for her grave is too characteristic to be omitted— "Her great and loving heart, her noble soul, her clear, powerful, original, and comprehensive intellect, made her the guide and support, the instructor in wisdom and the example in goodness, as she was the sole earthly delight of those who had the happiness to belong to her. As earnest for all public good as she was generous and devoted to all who surrounded her, her influence has been felt in many of the greatest improvements of the age, and will be in those still to come. Were there even a few hearts and intellects like hers, this earth would already become the hoped-for heaven." These lines proved the intensity of Mill's feeling, which is not afraid of abundant verbiage; but they also prove that he could not imagine what the effect would be on others, and, as Grote said, only Mill's reputation could survive these and similar displays.

It is impossible to omit all reference to this singular page in Mill's history. But it is possible to limit curiosity

* See Dr. Garnett's *Life of Carlyle*, p. 76.

to the psychological interest, beyond which all discussion
on such a matter is sheer impertinence. We have no
desire, as we have no right, to know any of the incidents
in detail of the long companionship; the bare outline of the
facts, in the general summary which has just been given,
is sufficient to show the strange influence to which Mill
was subjected for more than twenty years of his life.
The paradox of the situation is that Mill's character has
been generally regarded as somewhat cold and impassive:
a character, therefore, in which it was antecedently
improbable that we should find anything of the nature of
a romance. As a matter of fact, he had a considerable
depth of feeling, which was hidden behind a mask of icy
reserve; he was not deficient by any means in sentiments and emotions of a warm and generous character.
But if we may judge from his published writings, he
habitually underrated the strength of passion as it
exists in the majority of men; and this characteristic,
while it serves as a useful commentary to such events as
the foreign tour undertaken in companionship with Mrs.
Taylor, at the same time increases the marvel of Mill's
infatuation. For infatuation it can only be called when
a man of Mill's intellectual eminence allows himself to
describe his friend in terms of such unbounded adula-
tion—"Were I but capable of interpreting to the world
one half the great thoughts and noble feelings which are
buried in her grave, I should be the medium of a greater
benefit to it than is ever likely to arise from anything
that I can write, unprompted and unassisted by her
all but unrivalled wisdom." A man of common sense
and worldly judgment would be glad if such Ciceronian
phrases could only be accompanied by the Ciceronian

comment which the Roman orator made in one of his letters to Atticus—"*Nosti illas* ληκίθους."*

But we must be careful not to exaggerate the paradox. History gives us illustrative examples of philosophic weakness. Auguste Comte had his Clotilde, and Descartes his Princess Elizabeth ; and though such instances are not exactly parallel, they may serve to bring out a habitual feature in such relationships. To a man whose range of thought usually lies in the spheres of the abstract and the purely logical, there is a strange fascination in the lively presentation of the concrete and the practical. The latter faculty is so far denied to him that he tends to overestimate its importance. It seems like a revelation from another world if a woman of wit and imagination can clothe with living and palpable flesh some of those arid skeletons among which his mind has had to make its home. If we look at Carlyle's descriptive adjectives, " vivid " and " iridescent," there may be some indication conveyed of a picturesque and graphic power in dealing with concrete images, possessed by Mrs. Taylor, which doubtless would be attractive to Mill. He had been, as we have seen, a friend of Sterling, who possessed some of this power : at all events, Sterling's remark is significant, that Mill had singularly little sense of the concrete, and, though possessed of deep feeling, had little poetry. Perhaps Mrs. Taylor supplied him with both necessaries ; perhaps, as Dr. Garnett has suggested, it was due to her that Mill wrote his appreciative notice of Tennyson. As to the practical tendency, Mill himself has given evidence that it was exactly in this region that she was of such service to him. If there

* *Cic. Att.* I., 14. 3.

was any immediate relation to practice in his *Political Economy*, as distinguished from the writings of other economists, he declared that the praise should be hers.

No stress should probably be laid on an explanation which naturally rises to the lips of a worldly and half-cynical critic, that Mrs. Taylor flattered Mill by serving as an echo to his own opinions. Mill doubtless was above all coarse forms of flattery; and his friendship with and appreciation of such men as Sterling and Thornton sufficiently prove that his confidence was not always given to those only who agreed with him. Yet there is a common mistake which is made by men in their relation to clever women, which in part may have been present in this case. When a clever woman gives expression to some of the thoughts which, in the man's case, are the result of hard thinking, he is apt to imagine that she, too, must have been through a similar mental discipline, and that there is as much behind her expression of the thought as there would be if he had made use of it. A man habitually underrates the woman's quickness of apprehension, and her delicate and intuitive insight into some of the problems with which he has been wrestling. He admires her, therefore, in proportion to the seriousness of his own logic, not in reference to her own native powers. Such an explanation, however, would not be accepted by Mill himself, for he always believed that the characters of men and women were identical—an opinion which, be it true or false, would itself support some such delusion as that which has been traced above. It is, at least, a fact, that the feminine mind is surprisingly quick in assimilating and reproducing thoughts and ideas which have been sympathetically presented to it. It can adapt itself, perhaps, with greater readiness than the average masculine intellect to a new medium. Even if this be only a difference between two classes of mind rather than a difference between the sexes, its value as a possible key to Mill's reverential attitude is not impaired.

It may be remembered that Mill had had a training which was, in some respects, one of peculiar sadness. Whatever other effects James Mill's stern methods might be supposed to have produced, they certainly rendered his son an isolated and solitary being. The feeling crops up here and there in many parts of the *Autobiography.* He was not like other boys, and he could not, therefore, be their friend ; he had thoughts to which average men had no access ; above all, he had views on religion which tended to keep him away from his fellows. His acute and friendly observer at Falmouth, Caroline Fox, guessed that he was much alone. "He is," she wrote, "in many senses isolated, and must sometimes shiver with the cold."* If to this we add the rich endowment of feeling which Mill must have inherited from his mother, just as he inherited from her his aquiline features, and the iron restraint which he had been taught to impose upon all such "weaknesses" by his father, is his infatuation so strange ? It is the solitary men who surprise their contemporaries by unexpected outbursts ; it is the repression of feeling which often brings in its train some emotional conflagration. When Mill met Mrs. Taylor, all the hidden fire of affection which smouldered beneath a cold exterior rose to the surface. Is it curious that the lava-stream should have swept away some of the logical

* Caroline Fox's *Journals,* ii., 270.

judgment? Yet, if such explanations do not make it
clear why Mill's sentiments should have degenerated into
sentimentality, we can only fall back upon that subtle
sense of difference in mind, character, and experience
which, even in those who are exempt from what we
euphemistically call "romance," serves to make intellectual companionship between men and women at once
so great and so bewildering a stimulus.

It still remains to estimate the extent to which Mrs.
Taylor, both before and after her marriage with Mill,
made actual contributions to his thoughts and his published works. And here Mill gives us abundant help in
the *Autobiography*. When first he knew her, his thoughts
were turning to the subject of Logic. But his published
work on the subject owed nothing to her, he tells us, in
its doctrines. It was Mill's custom to write the whole of
a book so as to get his general scheme complete, and
then laboriously to re-write it in order to perfect the
phrases and the composition. Doubtless Mrs. Taylor
was of considerable help to him as a critic of style. But
to be a critic of doctrine she was hardly qualified. Mill
has some clear admissions on this point. "The only
actual revolution which has ever taken place in my
modes of thinking was already complete,"* he says,
before her influence became paramount. There is a
curiously humble estimate of his own powers (to which
Dr. Bain has called attention), which reads at first sight
as if it contradicted this. "During the greater part of
my literary life I have performed the office in relation to
her, which, from a rather early period, I had considered
as the most useful part that I was qualified to take in the

* *Autobiography*, p. 190.

domain of thought, that of an interpreter of original thinkers and mediator between them and the public." So far it would seem that Mill had sat at the feet of his oracle; but observe the highly remarkable exception which is made in the following sentence :—" For I had always a humble opinion of my own powers as an original thinker, *except in abstract science (logic, metaphysics, and the theoretic principles of political economy and politics).*"* If Mill, then, *was* an original thinker in logic, metaphysics, and the science of economy and politics, it is clear that he had not learnt these from her lips. And to most men logic and metaphysics may be safely taken as forming a domain in which originality of thought, if it can be honestly professed, is a sufficient title of distinction.

Mrs. Taylor's assistance in the *Political Economy* is confined to certain definite points. The purely scientific part was, we are assured, not learnt from her. " But it was chiefly her influence that gave to the book that general tone by which it is distinguished from all previous expositions of Political Economy that had any pretension to being scientific, and which has made it so useful in conciliating minds which those previous expositions had repelled. This tone consisted chiefly in making the proper distinction between the laws of the Production of Wealth, which are real laws of nature, dependent on the properties of objects, and the modes of its Distribution, which, subject to certain conditions, depend on human will. . . . *I had, indeed, partially learnt this view of things from the thoughts awakened in me by the speculations of the St. Simonians;* but it was made a living principle, pervading and animating the

* *Autobiography*, p. 242.

book, by my wife's promptings."* The part which is
italicised is noticeable. Here, as elsewhere, Mill thinks
out the matter by himself; the concrete form of the
thoughts is suggested or prompted by the wife. Apart
from this "general tone," Mill tells us that there was
a specific contribution. "The chapter which has had a
greater influence on opinion than all the rest, that on the
Probable Future of the Labouring Classes, is entirely due
to her. In the first draft of the book that chapter did not
exist. She pointed out the need of such a chapter, and
the extreme imperfection of the book without it; she
was the cause of my writing it." From this it would
appear that she gave to Mill that tendency to Socialism
which, while it lends a progressive spirit to his speculations on Politics, at the same time does not manifestly
accord with his earlier advocacy of peasant proprietorships. Nor, again, is it, on the face of it, consistent with those doctrines of individual liberty
which, aided by the intellectual companionship of his
wife, he propounded in a later work. The ideal of
individual freedom is not the ideal of Socialism, just as
that invocation of governmental aid to which the
Socialist resorts is not consonant with the theory of
laisser-faire. Yet *Liberty* was planned by Mill and his
wife in concert. Perhaps a slight visionariness of
speculation was no less the attribute of Mrs. Mill than
an absence of rigid logical principles. Be this as it may,
she undoubtedly checked the half-recognised leanings of
her husband in the direction of Coleridge and Carlyle.
Whether this was an instance of her steadying influence,†

* *Autobiography*, pp. 246, 247.
† Cf. an instructive page in the *Autobiography*, p. 252.

or whether it added one more unassimilated element to Mill's diverse intellectual sustenance, may be wisely left an open question. We can not, however, be wrong in attributing to her the parentage of one book of Mill, the *Subjection of Women.* It is true that Mill had before learnt that men and women ought to be equal in legal, political, social, and domestic relations. This was a point on which he had already fallen foul of his father's Essay on Government. But Mrs. Taylor had actually written on this very point, and the warmth and fervour of Mill's denunciations of women's servitude were unmistakably caught from his wife's view of the practical disabilities entailed by the feminine position.

What his wife really was to Mill we shall, perhaps, never know. But that she was an actual and vivid force, which roused the latent enthusiasm of his nature, we have abundant evidence. And when she died at Avignon, though his friends may have regained an almost estranged companionship, Mill was, personally, the poorer. Into the sorrow of that bereavement we cannot enter : we have no right or power to draw the veil. It is enough to quote the simple words, so eloquent of an unspoken grief, " I can say nothing which could describe, even in the faintest manner, what that loss was and is. But because I know that she would have wished it, I endeavour to make the best of what life I have left, and to work on for her purposes with such diminished strength as can be derived from thoughts of her, and communion with her memory."

CHAPTER VII.

IT has been remarked that after the publication of the *Logic* and the *Political Economy* there was a partial failure of energy in Mill, and a comparative cessation from literary labour. But in the years which we have now reached there is a second harvest, an aftermath of intellectual toil, which, if it does not quite reach the level of the work of 1843 and 1848, at all events includes one work, *Liberty*, which is as likely to live as any of Mill's productions. It also includes Mill's chief contribution to Moral Philosophy in the tract on *Utilitarianism*, and his principal polemic, *The Examination of Sir W. Hamilton's Philosophy*. Nor is it less fruitful in political speculation, as evidenced not only in the *Thoughts on Parliamentary Reform* and the treatise on *Representative Government*, but also in the directly practical considerations suggested by the essays on the American civil war. At a time when a great deal of mistaken enthusiasm was expended on the Confederate cause, Mill stood conspicuously forth as the champion of the North in articles which he wrote in *Fraser's Magazine* and the *Westminster Review*. To these must be added an important article on John Austin in the *Edinburgh Review*, and the valuable papers on *Auguste Comte and Positivism*, which were collected and published in a volume in 1864. We have only space to notice such of these manifold labours as serve to throw additional light on Mill's character and his life.

The *Liberty*, Mill tells us, was more directly and literally the joint production of himself and his wife than anything else which bears his name. " I had first planned and written it as a short essay in 1854. It was in mounting the steps of the Capitol in January 1855 that the thought first arose of converting it into a volume. None of my writings have been either so carefully composed or so sedulously corrected as this. After it had been written, as usual, twice over, we kept it by us, bringing it out from time to time and going through it *de novo*, reading, weighing, and criticising every sentence. Its final revision was to have been a work of the winter of 1858-9, the first after my retirement, which we had arranged to pass in the South of Europe. That hope and every other were frustrated by the most unexpected and bitter calamity of her death. After my irreparable loss, one of my earliest cares was to print and publish the treatise, so much of which was the work of her whom I had lost, and consecrate it to her memory (1859). I have made no alteration or addition to it, nor shall I ever. Though it wants the last touch of her hand, no substitute for that touch shall ever be attempted by mine." The *Liberty*, then, is, by Mill's express words, immediately connected with that influence of his wife on his mind which the last chapter was occupied in discussing. It seems to have had very different effects on his different friends. Kingsley, who saw it first on the table in Parker's shop, sat down and read it through there and then, and said that it made him a clearer-headed, braver-minded man on the spot. Caroline Fox held another opinion. "I am reading," she says, in a letter to E. T. Carne, "that terrible book of John Mill's on Liberty, so clear and calm and cold; he lays it on one as a tremendous duty to get oneself well contradicted, and admit always a devil's advocate into the presence of your dearest, most sacred truths, as they are apt to grow windy and worthless without such tests, if, indeed, they can stand the shock of argument at all. He looks you through like a basilisk, relentless as Fate. We knew him well at one time, and owe him very much. I fear his remorseless logic has led him far since then. No, my dear, I don't agree with Mill, though I, too, should be very glad to have some of my 'ugly opinions' corrected, however painful the process; but Mill makes me shiver, his blade is so keen and so unhesitating."

In one sense the book has a permanent value, and has largely entered into the life and thought of the present generation; in another sense its value is relative merely, because it belongs in spirit to the first rather than the last half of the nineteenth century. It is a reasoned defence of Individualism as an element of absolute and paramount importance in a state and in society, founded, as Mill himself admits, on the work of Wilhelm von Humboldt, who supplies the text, as the dedication to Mill's wife forms the preface of the treatise. It is a kind of philosophic text-book (again to avail ourselves of Mill's own statements) of "a single truth, which the changes progressively taking place in modern society tend to bring out into even stronger relief: the importance, to man and society, of a large variety in types of character, and of giving full freedom to human nature to expand itself in innumerable and conflicting directions." It therefore discusses and defends the individual right to Freedom of Discussion and Freedom of Action, and confines within narrow limits the right of Society to control or to punish. As a vindication of such views, the *Liberty*, doubtless, has great and lasting value. But so far. as it confuses character with eccentricity, so far as it belongs to the combative, negative spirit of revolt, rather than to the positive, constructive spirit of organised reform ; so far it shares the fate of the old *laisser-faire* doctrine of political economy, and is out of harmony with the tendencies and the ideas of the modern age. We have advanced fast and far in the last thirty years, and organisation and synthesis are our mottoes rather than atomism and individuality. Herbert Spencer is indeed an exception, but in times of change the best men are found on both sides of the dividing line.

The treatise on Liberty is written under certain presuppositions which tend to vitiate some of its conclusions. One of the results of Mill's so-called mental crisis was that he began to recognise the value of opposite and contradictory opinions. As a corrective against bigotry it is a valuable principle to assert the necessity of examining theories which do not accord with one's own. But it is another and a different principle to justify the necessity of such examination by the doctrine that truth lies half-way between two antithetical theories. Such a doctrine might be plausibly urged as an engine against dogmatism, but its value ceases when from a sword of offence and controversy it is beaten into a ploughshare of peace and domestic economy. For it is clearly impossible to have settled convictions, unless we may assume that some things may be taken for granted amongst reasonable people. It is certain that no amount of discussion will improve our belief in scientific dogmas ; for instance, that the world goes round the sun. It is more than doubtful whether even practical principles can be discussed without a very real danger. Does anyone really suppose, to take a recent contemporary instance, that we get a firmer hold on the arguments which prove the advisability of Marriage as a social institution by reading the interminable discussions in a morning paper as to whether marriage is a failure? In such matters, freedom of discussion, the free play of thought, which is recommended with regard even to our cherished convictions, is a very dubious blessing.

In reality the vindication of the claims of Individualism issues from an eighteenth-century delusion on the subject of "natural rights of man as man." If every individual has, as such, natural rights, it is clear enough why no amount of social stability can compensate for the infringement or limitation of such natural rights. In Mill, of course, the argument is not based on a fiction like this ; individual liberty is discussed on the grounds of its expediency. But when once divorced from the doctrines of the followers of Rousseau, the argument loses a great deal of its force, if, indeed, it is not fatally impaired. For the appeal to social expediency very often entails a verdict which is inconsistent with individual rights, and which, therefore, defeats the purpose of those who made the appeal. If Society be the ultimate arbiter, the individual must yield. Nor does Mill altogether escape from another eighteenth-century burden in his distinction between self-regarding acts and social acts. The argument is that society has no right to interfere in such things as only concern the individual. But directly the attempt is made to act on such a distinction, it becomes clear that the distinction itself cannot be maintained. It is impossible to draw a hard and fast line between conduct which only affects oneself and conduct which affects others. Indeed, the distinction itself appears to be the issue of the exploded fallacy of the social contract. Before the contract was made, man was only responsible to himself: after its enactment, he becomes responsible both to himself and to that state which his contract has created. But we no longer believe in the social contract theory, and the difference between self-regarding and social acts should be equally relegated to the limbo of detected impostures.

To us, at any rate (and this is the last point on which we need insist), it is becoming habitual to consider Society as logically prior to the Individual. The tendency to Universalism, which has been so often noted in modern philosophic thought, just as it places Nature before man, and the Absolute Reason before the individual thinker, equally emphasises the authority of Society over the members which compose it. Mill's book on Liberty is in reality composed according to a different thesis. It implicitly asserts that the Individual is logically prior to Society. In this matter Mill's speculations are completely in accord with that position which we have already seen him assume in his *Logic*. All knowledge depends on Experience, and experience is the experience of the individual. That experience should belong to the Race, and that in this position of subordination to the Race the individual should find some of his beliefs *à priori* to him, however much they may have been gathered out of the sensitive experience of his forefathers—this is a later doctrine than that which we find in Mill. And in the same fashion and to the same extent, later thought has modified the value of the individualistic doctrines of Mill's *Liberty.**

The other contributions which were made by Mill during these years to Political Philosophy need not occupy us long. *Thoughts on Parliamentary Reform* saw the light in the same year as *Liberty*, though parts of the pamphlet had been written some years previously. The immediate occasion of publication seems to have been the discussion on Lord Derby's and Mr. Disraeli's Reform Bill (1859); the principal features were hostility to the ballot, a claim of representation for minorities, and plurality of votes to be given, not to property, but to proved superiority of education. It was afterwards that Mill became acquainted with Mr. Hare's system of Personal Representation, for which he conceived a great admiration, and which he said he would have incorporated in his treatise had he been then aware of "so great a discovery in the political art." The hostility to the ballot he knew would form a point of difference between him and Grote : "Grote," he wrote in a letter, "knows that I now differ with him on the ballot, and we have discused it together, with no effect on either." This formed another of the opinions for which Mill was

* See p. 87 in the chapter on Mill's *Logic.*

indebted to his wife; but it was unfortunate, as Dr. Bain remarks, for Mill's political sagacity and prescience that the Legislature was converted to the ballot after he had abandoned it. In 1860 the volume on *Representative Government* was published, an important work, as containing in a connected form the various political doctrines to which he had at different times given expression. There is in it the same temperate discussion of the dangers of a Democracy which he had before adopted in his review of De Tocqueville and in essays in the *Westminster*, and a consideration of the proper relations between Order and Progress, to which he had been led by a study of Comte and the French political writers. Perhaps the most significant piece of political speculation is his distinction between the function of making laws and the function of getting good laws made. The first of these cannot be adequately performed by a numerous popular assembly, but the second cannot be satisfactorily fulfilled by any other authority. The consequence is, that in Mill's opinion there is " need of a Legislative Commission, as a permanent part of the constitution of a free country; consisting of a small number of highly-trained political minds, on whom, when Parliament has determined that a law shall be made, the task of making it should be devolved; Parliament retaining the power of passing or rejecting the bill when drawn up, but not of altering it otherwise than by sending proposed amendments to be dealt with by the Commission."

Although Mill does not deal with the question of a Hereditary Monarchy, it is of course known that he, as much as Grote, was a republican by principle; and in conversations with Bain he seems to have held that simple Cabinet Government was the natural substitute for Monarchy. In the concluding sentences of the book he takes occasion to advert to the India Bill, which abolished the East India Company. As a late official of that House, and the author of its protest against the proposed change, Mill naturally disliked the measure which removed him from his position, although privately he rejoiced at his own greater freedom and leisure. But his gloomy anticipations of the future of India, in consequence of the supercession of " John Company," have fortunately not been altogether realised. To the same period which produced *Liberty* and *Representative Government* can be also ascribed the publication of the first two volumes of Mill's *Dissertations and Discussions,* containing some of the best and most durable portions of his occasional work in the *Westminster* and *Edinburgh Reviews.*

More important for the estimation of Mill's thought and his position as a philosopher are the *Utilitarianism* and the *Examination of Sir W. Hamilton's Philosophy.* The *Utilitarianism* is a short collection of essays, originally brought out in *Fraser's Magazine,* which were published in book form in 1861. Hardly any book of Mill has been more fully canvassed and criticised. It is the principal contribution which Mill has made to the science of Ethics, and from this point of view it is, perhaps, a disadvantage that it should be so short and slight in its treatment. For Mill, in discussing the problems of morals, has assuredly raised more questions than he has answered, and made more enemies than friends. He did not please the Utilitarians of his day, who were formed in a narrower mould of thought than himself; still less could he satisfy those who belonged to a different school, to whom Utilitarianism and Empirical doctrines were altogether distasteful. Even his successors on scientific lines, who have entered into the heritage of the school to which he belonged, have been by no means reluctant to lay hands on their spiritual father. The reason is that here once again the cardinal characteristic of Mill, as a thinker, reappears—the desire to engraft on the older stock of Benthamism the blossoms of an alien growth. While the old foundation remains it is sometimes dangerous to add to the width of the superstructure; in philosophy, at all events, such lateral extension of dogmas only confuses the issue, and ends by discrediting that ground-plan which it was intended to justify.

Utilitarianism, as it was preached by Bentham, had the merits of precision and clearness. It might contain theories which were repugnant to cultivated and generous minds, but at least it was internally consistent, and presented an unbroken front to its assailants. The end of life was happiness, and happiness was ultimately the pleasurable consciousness of the individual. Moreover, the assumption was consistently maintained that the individual agent was animated by selfish motives, for Nature had placed mankind under the dominion of two masters, Pleasure and Pain, and it was for them to prescribe to the individual what he should do. Nor need there be any reasonable doubt as to what is or is not pleasure; for pleasure is only quantitatively estimable, and differences in kind between pleasures need not trouble the man who is aiming at the greatest sum of felicity. Mill, however, had sympathy with an opposite school, which maintained that other elements ought to be incorporated into an adequate scheme of human nature. His broad and tolerant mind desired to find room for some of their theories, as implicity contained in or reasonably deducible from his own inherited theories. According to the principles laid down in his *Liberty*, he had to admit "a devil's advocate" into the presence of his most cherished convictions. The result is that while Mill's treatise presents that refined and softened form of Utilitarianism which distinguishes it from the moral theory of the eighteenth century, it is by no means so internally coherent as the elder scheme, while it still falls short of the rational Utilitarianism which is based on Evolution, and professed, among others, by Mr. Herbert Spencer.

Only a few points can here be adverted to. If Happiness be the end of life, we have a right to a clear and precise statement of what Happiness means, and what it includes. But Mill is singularly vacillating on this point. Sometimes Happiness (as in the earlier part of the treatise) is simply identified with pleasure. Then appears the doctrine that happiness may exist without contentment, which interferes with its identification with pleasure. A "sense of dignity" is declared to be a part of happiness, and happiness means a desirable kind of life. It is further declared to have "ingredients," and appears not to be a mere "aggregate" or collective something. Thus gradually it has ceased to mean pleasurable emotion; it becomes the preferable or admirable life, and the "greatest happiness" that we have to seek is the realisation of a high and intense ideal.*

* See Bradley's *Ethical Studies*, p. 109.

Further, if in morality we are to aim at the greatest sum of pleasures, whether for ourselves or for humanity at large, we must know the intrinsic or extrinsic differences between pleasures. Do pleasures differ in kind, or only in amount? The earlier answer to this question was tolerably clear. Pleasures differ in amount, for quantity of pleasure being equal, said Bentham, pushpin is as good as poetry. But Mill will not commit himself to such barbarism as this. He knows that his own pleasures may perhaps not be relatively so large in amount as those of the sensualist, but that they are far higher in quality. Consequently, he admits that pleasures differ in quality, and, to this extent, puts himself right with that common-sense judgment which the narrower forms of Hedonism had outraged. But a logical difficulty remains. If pleasure be the test of morality, then, when we use the terms "higher" or "lower" pleasures, we must not refer to any other standard than that which our emotional test can justify. But inasmuch as the intellectual pleasure, for instance, which we call "higher," does not give us a greater amount of emotional gratification, but rather less, than the pleasure of the sensualist, we must, in using such terms as "higher" and "lower," be appealing to some other standard than that of feeling. In other words, a distinction in quality between pleasures *can* be made if our standard of estimation be something other than feeling, but *can not* be made, if we remain true to the psychological theory of Bentham. In this instance, as in many others, Mill has included in his scheme a distinction which his ground-plan does not admit of.

Again, is man originally a wholly selfish creature?

Yes, and no. If we analyse "Conscience" (which Mill treats as an acquired product, not as a primitive possession), we find that a series of associated ideas has gathered round an originally selfish germ. But the great support of our moral ideas is, we are told, the social feelings of mankind. These social feelings are, of course, in their nature sympathetic, and as such, are not selfish, but altruistic. Hence it would appear either that sympathy is originally selfish (which Mill never states and would hardly admit), or else that mankind have primitive feelings of altruism, and are not only inspired by a single regard, each for his own personal interests. Other difficulties surround Mill's account of the ultimate sanction of morality, and the proof of which the principle of Utility is susceptible ; but we have no space to refer to them here. How little the Evolutionists can accommodate themselves to Mill's position can be seen not only in Mr. Herbert Spencer's *Data of Ethics,** but also in Mr. Leslie Stephen's *Science of Ethics.* A reference to the latter work admirably illustrates the difference in presupposition and doctrine. According to Mr. Leslie Stephen,† Utilitarianism appears to assume that there is an uniform man, a colourless sheet of paper, a primitive atom, upon whom all qualities are imposed by the circumstances under which he is placed. Further, according to this doctrine, society is an aggregate, built up of the uniform atoms called men. Each of these desires happiness, and so happiness is regarded as a kind of emotional currency capable of being calculated and distributed in lots ;

* Cf. esp. *Data of Ethics*, pp. 220 and foll. (Edition of 1879.)
† L. Stephen, *Science of Ethics*, pp. 359 et foll.

and conduct is immoral or moral according as it diminishes or swells the volume of this hypothetical currency. The fundamental error here is the inability to understand the value of time, the meaning of development, and the consequent innateness (at least for the modern man) of certain tendencies of character, to which must be added the misunderstanding of the true nature of society, which is in many senses a living and growing organism, and not a concourse of independent atoms.*

In the same year in which the *Utilitarianism* was published (1861), Mill turned his thoughts to a criticism of Sir W. Hamilton's philosophy, but he interrupted his work on the subject, not only by a tour in Greece and Asia Minor in the summer of 1862, but also by his articles on the American War and on Comte, which have been already alluded to. As his reading in Hamilton progressed, he was increasingly struck by the inconsistencies which betrayed themselves in the Hamiltonian scheme of Metaphysics and Logic. "I was not prepared," he wrote to Bain, "for the degree in which this complete acquaintance lowers my estimate of the man and of his speculations. I did not expect to find them a mass of contradictions. It almost goes against me to write so complete a demolition of a brother-philosopher after he is dead, not having done it while he was alive." The volume (for he soon discovered that the article which he had originally projected did not give him adequate scope for his treatment) appeared in 1865. It is much more than a mere criticism of another system of

* Perhaps I may be permitted to refer for further details on Utilitarianism to my volume on *Constructive Ethics*, pp. 135-164.

thought. It makes definite contributions to a constructive system on empirical lines. As Mill himself said, it
enabled him to supply what was left deficient in the
Logic, and to do the kind of service to "rational" psychology of which he was capable—to write its *Polemik.*
Perhaps the most interesting and suggestive chapters are
chapters xi., xii., and xiii., which deal respectively with
our belief in an external world, our belief in self, and our
belief in the primary attributes of matter. Especially
acute and searching is his analysis of the steps by which
we gradually form the conception of a great material world
outside us. Starting from the changing sensations of the
present, we are led to the idea of a permanent background to present sensation in possible sensation, and
this background is then looked upon as a cause, of
which any given present sensation is the effect. Matter
itself can only be defined as the Permanent Possibility of
Sensation—a definition which shows Mill's complete
acceptance of the theory of Berkeley. Indeed, more
than half of the interest of these chapters is the near
approach which Mill makes to the position of Idealism,
which resolves all our notions of the external world into
the subjective affections of the thinking self. But the
point is too intricate to be indicated by merely passing
references, as it opens up the whole question of the
metaphysical basis of Mill's philosophy, and the exact
value of that intermediate position which he consciously
or unconsciously assumed between the Empiricism of
Locke and Hume, and the Idealism of the German
school.

The more strictly polemical portions of the book are very
effective, especially against the so-called "philosophy of

the conditioned," as professed by Hamilton and Mansel. Indeed, it may be suspected that it was Mansel's application of the doctrine to Religious Thought in his celebrated "Bampton Lectures" which gave a keener zest to Mill's critical ardour. In private conversation, he called Mansel's *Limits of Religious Thought* a "loathsome" book. For it seemed to make the God whom we describe by our moral terms exempt from the ordinary rules of our morality. If all the qualities we give to God have meaning only in reference to ourselves, and have no meaning in reference to God, such a doctrine does not put God above us, but in reality below the best level of our nature. Mill's style rises to an unusual height of emotional eloquence as he stigmatises this theory. The passage, which may be found in the seventh chapter of the *Examination*, ends with the famous climax, which was posted in large letters over the hoardings of Westminster, when Mill became a parliamentary candidate : "If such a being can sentence me to hell, to hell I will go." Mansel called this an exhibition of taste and temper ; Grote called it a Promethean defiance of Jove ; it at least served his political adversary as a convenient text for party polemics.*

It is pleasant in the midst of these literary toils to catch a glimpse of Mill's life at Avignon, and to discover

* Dr. Bain, in his *J. S. Mill*, p. 122, has the following curious note :—"Grote thought that the phrase was an echo of something occurring in Ben Jonson ; where a military captain's implicit obedience is crowned by the illustration—'Tell him to go to hell, to hell he will go.' I have never got any clue to the place." The line, of course, occurs in Johnson's "Vanity of Human Wishes," "and bid him go to hell, to hell he goes," a translation of the phrase, "in cœlum jusseris, ibit," of Juvenal's Græculus esuriens.

that he had quite regained the natural buoyancy of his spirits. "Life here," he wrote to his friend Thornton in 1861, "is uneventful, and feels like a perpetual holiday. It is one of the great privileges of advanced civilisation, that while keeping out of the turmoil and depressing wear of life, one can have brought to one's door all that is agreeable or stimulating in the activities of the outward world, by newspapers, new books, periodicals, etc. It is, in truth, too self-indulgent a life for anyone to allow himself whose duties lie among his fellow-beings, unless, as is fortunately the case with me, they are mostly such as can be better fulfilled at a distance from their society, than in the midst of it."

CHAPTER VIII.

(1865–1868.)

IN the celebrated allegory of the Cave, in Plato's
Republic, an account is given of the philosopher, who
had attained to the beatific vision, coming back again
to the old home of darkness, and with pain and difficulty
striving to discern in the company of his fellow-prisoners
the fleeting shadows on the wall. "Is there anything
surprising," asks Plato, "in one who passes from divine
contemplations to the evil state of man, misbehaving
himself in a ridiculous manner? If, while his eyes are
blinking, and before he has become accustomed to the
surrounding darkness, he is compelled to fight in courts
of law, or in other places, about the images or shadows
of images of justice, and is endeavouring to meet the
conceptions of those who have never yet seen the
absolute justice? Any one who has common sense will
remember that the bewilderments of the eyes are of two
kinds, and arise from two causes, either from coming out
of the light or from going into the light, which is true of
the mind's eye quite as much as of the bodily eye; and

he who remembers this when he sees any one whose vision is perplexed and weak, will not be too ready to laugh; he will first ask whether that soul of man has come out of the brighter life, and is unable to see because unaccustomed to the dark, or having turned from darkness to the day is dazzled by excess of light. And he will count the one happy in his condition and state of being, and he will pity the other; or, if he have a mind to laugh at the soul which comes from below into the light, there will be more reason in this than in the laugh which greets the other coming from above into the den."* The time had now come for Mill to enter public life; and if he too may have seemed to have had "a weak and perplexed vision," perhaps the reason was that he had come out of the brighter life. Some of the contempt, some of the admiration, which he encountered in what he himself terms a "a less congenial task," may be at least understood if we bear in mind Plato's acute distinction between the two kinds of disordered vision. If the philosopher of Avignon was called to the House of Commons at Westminster, shall we say that he was dazzled by excess of light, or bewildered because unaccustomed to the darkness?

In a letter, kindly contributed to the present life of Mill by Mr. Gladstone, an unequivocal judgment is expressed on this point. "We well knew," Mr. Gladstone writes, "Mr. Mill's intellectual eminence before he entered Parliament. What his conduct there principally disclosed, at least to me, was his singular moral elevation. I remember now that at the time,

* Plato, *Republic*, §§ 517, 518. Jowett's Translation, vol. iii., 403-4.

more than twenty years back, I used familiarly to call
him the Saint of Rationalism, a phrase roughly and
partially expressing what I now mean. Of all the
motives, stings, and stimulants that reach men through
their egoism in Parliament, no part could move or even
touch him. His conduct and his language were, in this
respect, a sermon. Again, though he was a philosopher,
he was not, I think, a man of crotchets. He had, I
think, the good sense and practical tact of politics,
together with the high independent thought of a recluse.
I need not tell you," Mr. Gladstone adds, "that, for the
sake of the House of Commons at large, I rejoiced in his
advent, and deplored his disappearance. He did us all
good. In whatever party, whatever form of opinion, I
sorrowfully confess that such men are rare." Other
judgments, however, are not equally complimentary to
Mill. Some of his friends regretted his being in the
House for his own sake. They thought that he was not
great enough there as compared with his standing in the
intellectual world. He seemed to them to remain the
literary man, apart from the world and manners of
politics; and although his earnestness, his quick enthusiasm, and the transparency of his convictions were
readily acknowledged as impressive, there was somehow in their mind more the desire for his success than
any feeling that the success had been won. To the
Conservatives he was, of course, obnoxious; but even
his political allies sometimes must have repeated to
themselves the Tacitean maxim, *Omnium consensu capax
imperii nisi imperasset.* He was the natural leader
of Liberal thought; not in the House, but out of it.
"Saint of Rationalism," however, in Mr. Gladstone's

happy phrase, he remained. He had been declared to be Adam Smith and Petrarch rolled into one; and if he thus combined sentimentalism with the doctrines of political economy, he equally exhibited the cold clearness of the Rationalist thinker, tempered by the emotional warmth of high moral ideas.

He was invited to become a candidate for Westminster, early in 1865, by Mr. James Beal, acting on behalf of the Liberal members of the constituency. It was not the first invitation that Mill had received. More than ten years previously Mr. Lucas and Mr. Duffey offered to bring him into Parliament for an Irish county, in consequence of his opinions on the Irish Land Question; but as he was then an official in the India House, the offer had to be declined. In the present instance the circumstances were altered. Westminster had always an ambition to be represented by eminent men, and to the list of men of such different kinds of distinction as Sir Francis Burdett, Cochrane, Byron's friend Hobhouse, and Sir de Lacy Evans, it desired to add the name of John Stuart Mill. Moreover, it would accept Mill on his own terms. He wrote, on receipt of the offer of his supporters, a letter for publication, which he himself characterises as one of the frankest explanations ever tendered to an electoral body by a candidate. He told them that he had no personal wish to become a member of Parliament, and that, as he thought that no candidate ought either to canvass or to incur any expense, he could not consent to do either. He said that if he were elected he could not undertake to give any of his time and labour to their local interests. He announced that he would answer no question on the

subject of his religious opinions, and that it was his firm
persuasion that women were entitled to representation in
Parliament on the same terms with men.   "Nothing at
the time," says Mill, "appeared more unlikely than that
a candidate (if candidate I could be called) whose
profession and conduct set so completely at defiance all
ordinary notions of electioneering should nevertheless be
elected.   A well-known literary man was heard to say
that the Almighty himself would have no chance of being
elected on such a programme.   I strictly adhered to it,
neither spending money, nor canvassing, nor did I take
any personal part in the election, until about a week
preceding the day of nomination, when I attended a few
public meetings to state my principles and give answers
to any questions which the electors might exercise their
just right of putting to me for their own guidance;
answers as plain and unreserved as my address."*
Despite such disadvantages Mill was elected by a
majority of some hundreds over his Conservative com-
petitor.   One incident in the history of this election is
too interesting to be passed over.   At one of the
meetings, chiefly composed of the working classes, Mill
was asked whether he had ever written and published a
judgment on the working classes of England, that, though
they differed from those of other countries in being
ashamed of lying, they were generally liars.   The sentence
occurred in the *Thoughts on Parliamentary Reform*, and
Mill, without hesitation, at once answered in two words,
"I did."   Scarcely were the words out of his mouth
when vehement applause resounded through the whole
meeting.   The first working man who spoke after Mill's

* *Autobiography*, p. 283.

admission was Mr. Odger, and he said, amid cheers, that the working classes had no desire not to be told of their faults. They wanted friends, not flatterers, and felt under obligation to anyone who told them anything in themselves which he sincerely believed to require amendment. "A more striking instance," says Mill, "never came under my notice of what, I believe, is the experience of those who best know the working classes, that the most essential of all recommendations to their favour is that of complete straightforwardness; its presence outweighs in their minds very strong objections, while no amount of other qualities will make amends for its apparent absence."

The first session of Parliament in which Mill took a part was the last in the career of Lord John Russell. After the death of Lord Palmerston, Lord Russell was invited by the Queen to form a Government, in which Mr. Gladstone was Chancellor of the Exchequer and leader of the House of Commons, and Mr. Chichester Fortescue became Secretary for Ireland. It was rumoured that Mill was to be offered the Secretaryship for India, in consequence of his services at the India House, but this proved as baseless as many of the rumours which were floating at the time. The session of 1866 was that of the Cattle Plague, the Jamaica Commission, the Fenian troubles in Ireland, and the abortive Reform Bill, which ended in the overthrow of the Liberal Ministry. In all of these matters Mill bore his share. His first vote in the House was in support of an amendment in favour of Ireland, moved by an Irish member, for which only five English and Scotch votes were given; the other four, besides Mill's, being those of Mr. Bright,

Mr. M'Laren, Mr. J. B. Potter, and Mr. Hadfield. His first speech was in answer to Mr. Lowe's reply to Mr. Bright on the Cattle Plague Bill, and, as Mill himself says, "was thought to have helped to get rid of a provision in the Government measure which would have given to landholders a second indemnity, after they had already been once indemnified for the loss of some of their cattle by the increased selling price of the remainder." His second speech was on the proposal made on February 16th to suspend the Habeas Corpus Act in Ireland, in which his sympathy with the Irish brought him into so much disfavour that he resolved to allow some interval to elapse before addressing the House again. The ear of the House was, however, gained by a speech which he delivered in support of Mr. Gladstone's Reform Bill. That ill fated measure of 1866, which proposed to reduce the county franchise from £50 to £14, and the borough franchise from £10 to £7, apparently pleased its friends no more than it did its natural enemies, and only served as an occasion for Mr. Lowe's fitful brilliance and Mr. Bright's famous allusions to the Cave of Adullam. Mill supported the measure, especially defending the working classes from various aspersions which had been cast on them in the course of debate. He argued that the interests of the working class never could be fairly explained and discussed unless they had a larger and more direct representation. The example of the United States was sufficient to prove that the Democracy were neither obstinate nor unteachable, for it was his belief that working men would correct their faults more readily than any other class, when warned of them in a friendly and

sincere spirit. During a subsequent debate on the
Redistribution Bill, Mill was still more successful in an
answer to an attack made upon him by Sir John Pakington
for calling the Conservative party "the stupid party."
Admitting that the passage referred to was to be found
in his *Considerations on Representative Government,* he
proceeded to say, "I never meant to say that the
Conservatives are generally stupid. I meant to say that
stupid people are generally Conservative. I believe that
is so obviously and universally admitted a principle that
I hardly think any gentleman will deny it. Suppose any
party, in addition to whatever share it may possess of the
ability of the community, has nearly the whole of its
stupidity, that party must, by the law of its constitution,
be the stupidest party; and I do not see why honourable
gentlemen should see that position at all offensive to
them, for it ensures their being always an extremely
powerful party. I know I am liable to a retort, and an
obvious one enough; and as I do not wish to allow any
honourable gentleman the credit of making it, I make it
myself. It may be said that if stupidity has a tendency
to Conservatism, sciolism, or half-knowledge, has a
tendency to Liberalism. Something might be said for
that, but it is not at all so clear as the other. There is
an uncertainty about sciolists; we cannot count upon
them; and therefore they are a less dangerous class.
But there is so much dense, solid force in sheer stupidity,
that any body of able men with that force pressing
behind them may ensure victory in many a struggle, and
many a victory the Conservative party has gained
through that power." A short time afterwards the
Conservative party succeeded in ousting their rivals, and

Mr. Disraeli vindicated the truth of Mill's words by the necessity under which he lay of "educating his party."

The chief occasion during the session of 1866, on which Mill became at once notorious and unpopular, was the attempted prosecution of Governor Eyre for his conduct in the Jamaica insurrection. The insurrection had taken place in the preceding year; and though at first the majority of Englishmen congratulated themselves on the promptitude with which it had been stamped out, it was subsequently discovered with how much unnecessary violence and brutality the repressive measures had been executed. So high did the feeling run, that the Government felt themselves under the necessity of sending out a Royal Commission and relieving Eyre of his governorship. After the report of the Commission the excitement increased, for it became clear that, long after the insurrectionary movements of the negroes had subsided, there was an amount of hanging, flogging, and burning, which seemed to prove that the authorities had completely lost their heads. Men were flogged and hanged for no other reason than because they fell in the way of an excited soldiery, ripe for vindictive work; women were stripped and scourged under circumstances of the grossest cruelty. In all, four hundred and thirty-nine persons were put to death; over six hundred of both sexes were flogged. Especial suspicion attached to Governor Eyre for his conduct in putting to death Gordon, the supposed leader of the negro revolt; for the man had been arrested in Kingston, where no martial law had been proclaimed, and hurried off to Morant Bay, in order to come under the jurisdiction of martial law. The court-martial which tried him was in itself ridiculous;

it was composed of two young navy lieutenants and an ensign in one of the West India regiments. Yet it was under these circumstances, and by such a court as this, that Gordon was condemned to the fate which he subsequently suffered. Lord Chief-Justice Cockburn, in a celebrated charge which was soon after delivered to a grand jury, laid down his opinion of the matter in the following words :—"After a most careful perusal of the evidence which was adduced against him (Gordon), I come irresistibly to the conclusion that if the man had been tried on that evidence—I must correct myself; he could not have been tried upon that evidence; I was going too far, a great deal too far, in assuming that he could. No competent judge acquainted with the duties of his office could have received that evidence. Three-fourths, I had almost said nine-tenths, of the evidence upon which that man was convicted and sentenced to death, was evidence which, according to no known rules—not only of ordinary law, but of military law—according to no rules of right or justice, could possibly have been admitted; and it never would have been admitted, if a competent judge had presided, or if there had been the advantage of a military officer of any experience in the practice of courts-martial." Carlyle may have thought it right to be indignant with this charge; but it was an exposition of the laws of England, which was fatal to the credit of the authorities in Jamaica.

Two parties were formed in England on this question. One of them was in a fashion led by Carlyle, and received the support of Tennyson, Kingsley, and Ruskin, besides a number of Conservative politicians. The leaders of the other party were Mill and Herbert

Spencer, among philosophers; Bright, and other Liberal politicians; Professor Huxley, Mr. Frederick Harrison, and Mr. Goldwin Smith. A Jamaica Committee was formed by the latter party, of which the first chairman was Mr. Charles Buxton, and the second Mill himself. It is not necessary at the present day to recount in detail the arguments that were urged on both sides. It is clear enough that the plea of Carlyle, and all those who took up what was called the "damned nigger" view, was that, in a moment of general panic, Governor Eyre by his promptitude had saved the island. They did not deny that cruel acts had been committed; they only urged that it was better, even at the price of cruelty, to put down every chance of a general outbreak. The party led by Mill was, so far as we can see, animated by the purest motives. Whether they sufficiently estimated the conditions under which a government of Blacks by Whites has to be carried on is, perhaps, an open question; but there was no doubt that it was their chief desire to vindicate the fair fame of England from the stain of ferocious outrage. The late Professor Green of Oxford, himself a Humanitarian and a Moralist, once remarked that he would rather have been Mill than Carlyle, perhaps in reference to this very controversy. However unpopular Mill's activity against Governor Eyre might have made him at the moment, it is probable that most thinking men of the present day will consider that the part which he took in this matter is one of the chief evidences of the high moral spirit which animated him in his public life. His speech on this question in the House, when he moved that recent transactions in Jamaica required the investigation of a judical tribunal, was considered by Mill to have been his best Parliamentary speech.* He may not have been able to discern the shadows on the wall as well as some of the habitual denizens of the Cave, and he may have been wrong in pressing the matter, as he did, before the Law Courts. But the charge of the Chief-Justice of England remains as the best defence of the action of the Jamaica Committee, and the most damning piece of evidence against Eyre and his subordinates.

Another occasion on which Mill's name came before the public is less equivocal in its bearing on his fame. The Government of Lord Russell and Mr. Gladstone had been overthrown by a motion of Lord Dunkellin on the Reform Question, and had been succeeded by a ministry in which Lord Derby was Premier, and Mr. Disraeli Chancellor of the Exchequer. Some of the disappointed Reform Leaguers in London, incensed at this failure of a measure which was, at all events, intended to promote their wishes, determined to hold a meeting in Hyde Park. Their adviser and the president of the League was Mr. Edmond Beales, who appears to have been a man of some resolution. Mr. Walpole, the Home-Secretary, acting on behalf of the authorities, posted up a proclamation prohibiting the meeting. Whether it was legal or not to prevent the gathering was apparently somewhat of an open question; but the leaders of the Reformers, on being refused admittance into the Park, retired quietly enough to Trafalgar Square, and held a meeting there. Meanwhile, the crowd at the Park entrances, composed partly

* *Autobiography*, p. 298.

of sympathisers, partly of sightseers, being woefully
disappointed at the tameness of the issue, revenged
themselves by breaking down the iron railings, and,
despite the resistance of the police, careered over the
flower-beds through the greater part of the night. Next
morning Mr. Beales and his friends waited on Mr.
Walpole, and gravely expostulated with him, as though
he had been the sole cause of the disturbances of
the day before. Mr. Walpole was understood to have
melted into tears at the kindness of the Reformers, and
to have agreed that the right of meeting was to be tested
in a more satisfactory fashion at some future day.

And now Mill comes on the scene. He had already
in Parliament taken the side of the working-men in the
censure passed on the Home-Secretary, and asserted
that if the people had not the right to meet in the Park,
they ought to have it. He was now enabled to prove
himself the friend of the Reformers in still better fashion.
It must be remembered that the exasperation of the
working-men at the issue of the first conflict between
them and authority was extreme. "They showed," says
Mill, "a determination to make another attempt at a
meeting in the Park, to which many of them would
probably have come armed." The Government made
military preparations to resist the attempt, and something
very serious seemed impending. The sequel may be
told in Mill's words. "At this crisis I really believe that
I was the means of preventing much mischief. I was
invited, with several other Radical Members of Parliament, to a conference with the leading members of the
Council of the Reform League; and the task fell chiefly
upon myself of persuading them to give up the Hyde

Park project, and hold their meeting elsewhere. It was
not Mr. Beales and Colonel Dickson who needed
persuading; on the contrary, it was evident that these
gentlemen had already exerted their influence in the
same direction, thus far without success. It was the
working-men who held out, and so bent were they on
their original scheme that I was obliged to have recourse
to *les grands moyens.* I told them that a proceeding
which would certainly produce a collision with the
military could only be justifiable on two conditions—if
the position of affairs had become such that a revolution
was desirable, and if they thought themselves able to
accomplish one. To these arguments, after considerable
discussion, they at last yielded, and I was able to
inform Mr. Walpole that their intention was given up.
I shall never forget the depth of his relief, or the
warmth of his expressions of gratitude." Subsequently,
because Mill thought he owed them something for their
concessions on this occasion, he attended a meeting of
the Reform Leaguers, and spoke at the Agricultural Hall.
But he was never a member of the League. He disagreed
on two important points. He could neither believe in
the virtues of the ballot, nor could he accept the programme of manhood suffrage without considerable
limitations.

We now come to the session of 1867 and the Reform
Bill of the Conservative Government. It was the session
of the "leap in the dark"—the session in which Mr.
Disraeli so far educated his party as to make them accept
a measure which was considerably in advance of that
proposed in the preceding year. To the various changes
and ameliorations forced upon the Government, or

suggested by the Proteus-like Chancellor of the Exchequer, Mill contributed but little. He spoke on
May 2nd on the question of the Compound Householder,
that strange and irrepressible creature who so long vexed
the ingenuity of the House, and who was wittily described
by some member of the House as the male of the *femme
incomprise.* Mill supported an amendment of Mr.
Hibbert that householders under £10 should come in
on the same terms as the compound householders at or
above that amount; but the Government triumphed by
a majority of sixty-six. A more important contribution
to the debate was furnished later. Mill moved an
amendment on a favourite theme, which had often been
in his thoughts—the right of women to the vote. He
did not claim, he said, the vote for women as an abstract
right, but his argument was one of expediency and
justice. It was a doctrine of the British Constitution
that taxation and representation should co-exist; many
women paid taxes, and, therefore, should be allowed to
vote. There was evidence in our records that women, in
a distant period of our history, had voted for counties
and some boroughs, and there was no reason why they
should not vote now. Women, he submitted, ought no
longer to be classed with children and idiots and lunatics,
who needed to have everything done for them, but they
ought to be treated as equal in intelligence to, and having
equal rights with, men; and the disadvantages under
which they laboured with respect to the laws affecting
property, and the admission to professions, ought to be
removed. The amendment, which was at first treated in
a somewhat jocular spirit, was afterwards argued with
such earnestness that Mill induced seventy-three members

in all to vote for it. It was thrown out by a majority of
one hundred and twenty-three. At a subsequent period
Mill brought forward the question of the representation
of minorities, on the lines of Mr. Hare's plan, and
supported Mr. Lowe on the question of cumulative
voting. On these points he acted in complete conformity
with what he had put forward in his published writings.

Hardly any allusion has as yet been made to that
important sphere of Mill's activity in Parliament which is
concerned with the Irish question. It is, of course,
impossible, within the limits prescribed by this chapter, to
trace the course of the Fenian movement, together with
all the circumstances of tragi-comedy which followed in
its train. The eccentric career of James Stephens, the
fate of the " Phœnix " clubs, and all the mingled misery
and fortitude of the rising of the " bare-armed Fenians "
—to use the expression of Hector McIntyre in Scott's
Antiquary—are only of importance so far as they explain
and justify Mill's sympathetic energy. Early in the
session of 1866 the Habeas Corpus Act was suspended.
In the debate which preceded that suspension, Mill made
a speech in which he compared the action of the Government to that of the captain of a ship, or the master of a
school, who is for ever taking strong measures to preserve
discipline. In such cases the constant necessity for
strong measures proves that the system is wrong. Those,
on the contrary, who demand exceptional measures in
the treatment of Ireland are continually met with "the
eternal political *non possumus*" of English statesmen,
which in Mill's judgment only meant, " We don't do it in
England." A stronger speech followed subsequently on
a motion of the Irish Secretary, Mr. Fortescue, which

attempted to deal with the vexed relations between landlord and tenant in the Sister Isle. In this, which Mill calls "a careful speech" in his *Autobiography*, he argued on the same lines. The application of the same laws to England and Ireland, he said, showed that double ignorance which was older than the time of Socrates; the English not only did not know the people of whom they were talking, but they did not know themselves. The fact was that Ireland was not an exceptional country, but England was.. They ought to look to Continental experiences; and that told them that, wherever a system of agricultural economy like that in Ireland had been found consistent with the good cultivation of the land and the good condition of its peasants, rents had not been, as in Ireland, fixed by contract, but the occupier had had the protection of fixed usage, the custom of the country, and had had secured to him permanence of tenure so long as he pleased to possess it. The speech, together with one delivered some time afterwards, to which we shall presently refer, was published, not by Mill, but with his permission, in Ireland. Then in 1867 occurred the Fenian rising and the trials of the Fenian leaders. One of these, Colonel Burke, who had served with distinction in the ranks of the South in the American war, was sentenced to death in May. It was felt that in such a case justice might be mitigated with mercy, and in a great public meeting at St. James' Hall, Mill made a fine speech amidst the cheers of an audience composed almost entirely of English workmen. The orator was successful, and the sentence of death was remitted by Lord Derby.

The rescue of prisoners in Manchester and the

Clerkenwell explosion, towards the end of the same year, brought the Irish question once more to the front, and, as we now know, first induced Mr. Gladstone to enter upon his Irish legislation. Mill had written a pamphlet on *England and Ireland* in the winter of 1867, which was published early in the following year. In the session of 1868, when Mr. Disraeli became Prime Minister, on the retirement of Lord Derby, Mr. Maguire, one of the members for Cork, brought forward a motion on March 16th relative to the condition of Ireland, in which express mention was made of the "scandal and anomaly" of the Irish Church. A few days later Mill spoke. He began by regretting that nothing was to be done on the land question; but he specially regretted the determination not to deal with the State Church, an anomaly condemned by the whole human race, which no people would submit to but at the point of the sword. The taunt of Utopianism had been levelled at Mill, in consequence of his pamphlet and his known opinions on peasant-proprietorship in Ireland. He retorted that the proposal to endow the Roman Catholic clergy was "kakotopian," too bad to be put into practice—a frigidly academic phrase, which did not amuse the House. But the text of his discourse, that "large and bold measures alone could cure Ireland," was strikingly prophetic of what was to come in the following session.

There is no space to do more than mention other occasions on which Mill spoke. In the session of 1866 he made a powerful speech on the necessity of paying off the National Debt before the coal-fields were exhausted, in which occurred a fine passage on our duty to Posterity.

He also sat as one of a committee presided over by Mr. Ayrton, in reference to a proposed municipal government for the metropolis. In Mr. Disraeli's administration (1868) he opposed a motion to abolish Capital Punishments, and also spoke on the Election Petitions Bill. Lastly, on the question of the Alabama claims, he suggested, in support of Arbitration, that a mixed Commission should be appointed to ascertain the damages inflicted on the United States. Then came the celebrated resolutions on the Irish Church, proposed by Mr. Gladstone, which led to the dissolution of Parliament, and the general election in the winter. Mill was defeated at Westminster by Mr. W. H. Smith (who has since become leader of the House in the present Conservative Government), and immediately retired into seclusion at Avignon.

It is not difficult to find reasons for Mill's failure in 1868. Perhaps the constituency was tired of being represented by a philosopher; perhaps the philosopher himself had been guilty of eccentricity, which is so much graver a fault in a member than complacent stupidity. Certain it is that Mill had to some extent disappointed the expectations of his partisans, though it is by no means certain that those expectations were reasonable. He had, as he himself said, taken up the more recondite points of the Liberal creed, and hence was not in perfect sympathy even with the party with which he habitually acted. Above all, he had publicly sent a subscription to Mr. Bradlaugh's election expenses, which argued greater sympathy with working men's interests elsewhere than prudence in the case of his own interests at Westminster.

Many were sorry that he could not share in the fortunes of the Liberal Administration of 1869, especially those who cared for the higher moralities of public life. For Mill, at all events, was untouched by the wiles of that which a French writer calls "la politique, la grande suborneuse"—Politics the great corruptress; he had entered the arena of Politics, as men of the better sort usually do, with convictions, but, unlike them, had left with something higher than mere interests. Mr. Gladstone, who was bound in closer friendship with Mill than members of the House were generally aware of, was struck, as we have seen, with the singular moral elevation of his character. "He did us all good." But nature had evidently not intended Mill for a debater and an orator. The House listened to him with respect, but he seemed like a man who was performing a difficult and disagreeable duty in addressing it. He was hardly fluent, deliberating on every sentence, and though quite calm in manner, often pausing for some minutes for an appropriate phrase. Mr. Gladstone's judgment on this matter is final. In his letter, which was quoted at the commencement of this chapter, he praises Mill's mental faculty as a debater. But there was no warmth or contagiousness about Mill's oratory. "Physically, it came as from a statue."

CHAPTER IX.

WHILE Mill was in Parliament, the recess was his only opportunity for continuing his literary work. Thus, in the winter which succeeded his election at Westminster, he wrote a long article on Grote's *Plato and the other Companions of Socrates*, in preparation for which, in his usual laborious way, he studied the whole of Plato's works. He also brought out a new edition of his *Logic*, in which he added fresh examples to the inductive methods detailed in his third book, and argued for the first time against Spencer's " inconceivability of the opposite" as a test of truth. In the next recess, between 1866 and 1867, he wrote his address to the students of St. Andrews, who, without asking his leave, had elected him their Lord Rector. Dr. Bain, who speaks with some authority on such a question, says that this address was a failure. Mill, he says,* had no conception of the limits of a University curriculum. " At present the obligatory sciences [in the Scotch Universities] are Mathematics, Natural Philosophy, Logic, and Moral Philosophy. If he had consulted me on this occasion, I should have endeavoured

* Bain : *J. S. Mill*, p. 127.

to impress upon him the limits of our possible curriculum, and should have asked him to arbitrate between
the claims of Literature and Science, so as to make the
very most of our time and means.   He would then have
had to balance Latin and Greek against Chemistry,
Physiology, and Jurisprudence, for it is quite certain that
both these languages would have to be dropped absolutely
to admit his extended science course."   But Mill was
doing more than merely addressing a Scotch audience ;
he was drawing a picture of the whole of the Higher
Education.   Perhaps Dr. Bain is wounded by Mill's
resolute vindication of the importance of Greek and
Roman classics, for half the address is occupied with
this subject, on which he had already given his opinion
in his article on De Tocqueville.*   The series of the
sciences is discussed in accordance with the scheme of
Comte.   Amongst other noticeable passages he introduced one on the subject of free-thought, which seems
especially to have pleased the St. Andrews students.

In the recess of 1867 he was busy with his edition of
James Mill's *Analysis of the Human Mind,* which was
published in 1869.   The work, which was called by Mill
" a duty to philosophy and to the memory of my father,"
was undertaken conjointly by Dr. Bain, Mr. Grote, and
Dr. Andrew Findlater, with Mill himself as editor.   Mill
found this occupation a very great relief "from its
extreme unlikeness to parliamentary work, and to
parliamentary semi-work or idleness."   "Admirably
adapted," he says, "for a class-book of the Experience
Metaphysics, it only required to be enriched, and in
some cases corrected, by the results of more recent

* *Dissertations and Discussions,* vol. ii., p. 69, note.

labours in the same school of thought, to stand, as it now does, at the head of systematic works on Analyic Psychology." The most remarkable publication belonging to the year 1867[*] is, however, the *Subjection of Women*, of which portions were written by Miss Helen Taylor, while Mill's share was the result of discussions and conversations with his wife. With the possible exception of the *Utilitarianism*, there is no work of Mill which has been more abundantly criticised than this. Even his friends thought its argument was overstrained ; for it has a depth and intensity of passion in the language which could only be understood if the author were advocating divorce, pure and simple, in the case of ill-assorted unions. But this is exactly what Mill does not do. The argument proceeds on the following principles : equality is itself the highest expediency, and the burden of proof must always lie on those who maintain inequality. Justice, in fact, requires that all people should live in society as equals. Moreover, history shows that progress has been from a law of force to a condition in which command and obedience become exceptional. Finally, the law of the strongest having been abandoned in this country, it ought not to apply to the relation between the sexes. Now it is obvious that none of these propositions are axiomatic ; they can be, and have been, impugned in detail by many thinkers and critics. No discussion on this subject equals in vigour Sir Fitzjames Stephen's attack in his *Liberty, Equality, Fraternity.*[†] The critic

---

[*] In the same year were published *Endowments* and *Labour and its Claims*, a review of Thornton's work.

[†] *Liberty, Equality, Fraternity.* By James Fitzjames Stephen, Q.C. Pp. 203, et foll.

admits that there are cases in which men have abused their power, as, for instance, in the "stupid coarseness" of the laws about the effects of marriage on property, but while he believes that all Societies ultimately rest on force, he does not conceal his disbelief in the natural equality of individuals. It is needless to repeat arguments which have been abundantly thrashed out in contemporary discussions. But there is one simple principle which must largely affect our view on the possible equality of men and women. Nature has prescribed to woman specific functions, which, as they are exhaustive to her powers, must leave her unequal to man in vigour, unless she has been originally furnished with greater chances of success in the struggle of life. Can anyone assert that she starts stronger than man? And, if not, how can she, being what she is, ever be his equal?

It is more interesting and more profitable to pass from such contested points to the remaining incidents of Mill's life. In 1869 he meditated, we are told, writing a book on Socialism,* and he was busy with peasant proprietorships and the "unearned increment" in his studies on the Land Question. The last public work in which he was engaged was the starting of the Land Tenure Reform Association, in favour of which he made a public speech only a few months before his death. We get a pleasant picture of his cottage life at Avignon in a letter he wrote to his friend Thornton. "Helen [Miss Helen Taylor, his step-daughter] has carried out her long-cherished scheme (about which she tells me she consulted you) of a 'vibratory' for me, and has made a

* See "Chapters on Socialism," *Fortnightly Review*, 1879.

pleasant covered walk, some thirty feet long, where I can vibrate in cold or rainy weather. The terrace, you must know, as it goes round two sides of the house, has got itself dubbed the 'semi-circumgyratory.' In addition to this Helen has built me a herbarium, a little room fitted up with closets for my plants, shelves for my botanical books, and a great table whereon to manipulate them all. Thus, you see, with my herbarium, my vibratory, and my semi-circumgyratory, I am in clover; and you may imagine with what scorn I think of the House of Commons, which, comfortable club as it is said to be, could offer me none of these comforts, or more perfectly speaking, these necessaries of life."* Mill, as we have said before, was an enthusiastic botanist, and during his last journey to Avignon he was looking forward with keen interest to the spring flowers.

In 1871 his own and his father's friend, Grote, died, and was buried in Westminster Abbey. Mill disliked this public interment, but could not refuse to attend the funeral and walk as one of the pall-bearers. Dr. Bain says that as he and Mill walked out from the ceremony, Mill made the remark—" In no very long time I shall be laid in the ground with a very different ceremonial from that." In this year he was only sixty-seven, but he felt that he had taxed his energies to the full, and that the end could not be far off. Several attacks of illness he bore with patience during the next two years, and a few days before his actual death he made a long botanical excursion. But a local endemic disease proved fatal, and he died on May 8th, 1873. There is an interesting note in Dr. Bain's book as

* Quoted by Professor Minto in *Encycl. Brit.*, vol. xvi.

to Mill's funeral. It seems that Mill had made a friend of the Protestant pastor at Avignon, who was an intelligent and liberal-minded man. The pastor ventured to offer up a prayer over Mill's grave, and thereby got into trouble, and had to write a letter in the local newspapers excusing himself for this act of consideration on behalf of a notorious sceptic. It is a satisfaction to know that Mill died with his faculties clear. His favourite text had been "the night cometh when no man can work," and on the night of his death, when he was informed that he would not recover, he said simply, "My work is done." Few men had better reason to express so calm a confidence.

The *Autobiography*, part of which had been written in 1861, and part after 1870, came out after his death, and enabled all men to understand how serious and simple had been the life of the man who had died so calmly. The other posthumous work, *Essays on Religion*, caused more commotion, and renewed many of the controversies which had existed during his lifetime as to his real convictions. To some the book came as a disappointment, to others as a relief, to all as a surprise. But while it renders still more difficult the task of reconciling the various items of Mill's creed, it must be remembered that the third essay, at all events, is only a first draft, and had not the benefit of that careful revision which Mill was in the habit of giving to all that he published on his own authority.

"The two first of these three essays," says Miss Helen Taylor in her introductory notice, "were written between the years 1850 and 1858, during the period which intervened between the publication of the *Principles of Political Economy* and that of the work on *Liberty*. The last essay belongs to a different epoch. It was written between the years 1868 and 1870, but it was not designed as a sequel to the two essays which now appear along with it, nor were they intended to appear all together." It is important to remember these facts, for they serve to explain in some measure the divergence in view between the earlier and later portions of the volume—a divergence which we may take for granted, since so enthusiastic a disciple of Mill as Mr. Morley has taken pains to accentuate it in the articles which he wrote in the *Fortnightly Review.** The first essay has as its subject the various interpretations which may be given of the term Nature. Its purpose is to show that if "Nature" be taken as a guide either in religion or in morals, it is a term equally ambiguous and defective. We can neither construct an ethical theory on the ground of "conformity to Nature," as, for instance, the Stoics attempted, nor have we any justification for basing a religious creed on a consideration of natural processes. For the fact is, according to Mill, that Nature, as distinct from human activity and foresight, exhibits specimens of reckless violence and brutality which would be universally condemned according to any human standard. In a passage of great rhetorical energy Mill describes Nature as Tennyson describes her in his *In Memoriam :* " red in tooth and claw with ravine." All the good that has been done to the world and to humanity has been effected by human powers in limiting, controlling, and overpowering the blind and senseless havoc of natural forces. How, then, can a so-called "natural religion " be defensible? To argue from the signs and evidences

* *Fortnightly Review*, 1874, 1875.

of the natural world to its Creator, is to ascribe what is immeasurably below man to that which is, in the language of religious fervour, asserted to be infinitely above man. One of the hardest tasks which is assigned to the human race is the duty of reforming religion itself. The conclusion which Mill reaches is thus expressed*—" The only admissible moral theory of Creation is that the principle of good cannot at once and altogether subdue the powers of evil, either physical or moral; could not place mankind free from the necessity of an incessant struggle with the maleficent powers, or make them always victorious in that struggle, but could and did make them capable of carrying on the fight with vigour and with progressively increasing success. Of all the religious explanations of the order of nature, this alone is neither contradictory to itself nor to the facts for which it attempts to account." It must be admitted, however, that the value of the essay is much lessened by the fact that at the time at which it was composed, Darwin's newer view of nature was not fully before the world. Here, as elsewhere in Mill, we are to regard Nature on the ground of a conception based on individual experiences. Mill takes, as Mr. Morley terms it, merely the surface or horizontal view of Nature. The works of Darwin and Herbert Spencer enable us to substitute for this what may be called a transverse section of natural phenomena, whereby we can observe the successive layers of a historical development. One result of the latter view is effectually to reduce that power which Mill attributed to man, of altering or transforming the course of nature for his

* *Essays on Religion*, p. 39.

own and other's good : for man is shown to be swept along the current of natural forces, and to be himself a part of nature. This may or may not affect the general conclusions of the essay ; it obviously interferes with some of the arguments in detail.*

The second essay may be passed over with only a slight reference. It is on the Utility of Religion, and is, in Mr. Morley's summary, an attempt to answer the following questions :—Is religion of direct service to temporal interests, a direct instrument of social good? Is it useful in improving and ennobling individual human nature? If its utility in either of these two ways be allowed, must the form of religion be necessarily supernatural, involving a journey beyond the boundaries of the world which we inhabit, and beyond anything which could be supplied by the idealisation of our earthly life? In dealing with these questions, Mill's general contention is that religion is of considerable utility, but it need not be supernatural, nor deal with problems beyond the reach of human ken. But as we found that Mill's *Utilitarianism* was considerably embarrassed by the want of any clear conception of what happiness is, so his discussion of the present subject is hampered by a similar obscurity in his conception of religion. Religion is apparently a yearning to know whether our ideal and imaginative conceptions have realities answering to them in other worlds than ours. But the conclusion of the essay is that the

* The reader may be referred for an able polemic in favour of the religious view as against some of the inferences from Darwinism to Dr. James Martineau's *Study of Religion*, esp. vol. ii., pp. 270-397.

Positivist religion of Humanity, or as Mill prefers to call it, the religion of Social Duty, has all the value of the popular religion, as well as greater scientific certainty. Now, a religion of Humanity has clearly nothing to do with other worlds than ours. Hence some part, at all events, of the essence of religion is missed in that which Mill proposes to give as an entirely adequate substitute.

His object is, as we have said, to replace what is ordinarily termed Religion by the Positivist conception of a religion of Humanity. But the value and expediency of this substitution is rendered more than doubtful in the third essay. In the Essay on Theism there is sometimes the suggestion, sometimes the clear recognition, that what is valuable in religion (or, at all events, that which renders it valuable to the majority of mankind) is the element of wonder and mystery which encircles the problems with which it deals. With regard to three leading ideas—the idea of God as cause of the world, the idea of Christ as a divinely-appointed teacher, and the idea of immortality—Mill has considerations to offer which render them not indeed dogmas to be intellectually accepted, but hypotheses of some little probability, which may be defended on even scientific grounds. The ideas are not, it is true, such as they would be represented by the religious consciousness, but they are put forward in a sketchy, tentative fashion, as though most of the destructive portions of the two first essays had never been written. It is this playing with probabilities, this deliberate attempt to live in a twilight land of semi-faith, which caused so much consternation among those of Mill's disciples who had fed themselves on his

earlier work.   God is declared to be, though not
omnipotent, yet always benevolent; albeit that the main
object of the Essay on Nature was to show that natural
operations were replete with unreasoning cruelty.   There
is a shadow of chance that the soul may be immortal,
because the physical part of our thinking frame is only a
concomitant, not the cause of our mental life.*   Lastly,
if we select all those sayings of Christ which strike us as
of the highest value, and reject all those which appear to
be merely on the level or below the level of the morality of
his age, we are left with a character which is apparently
inexplicable on natural and historical grounds.   Yet
if there was one thing more than another which the
sixth book of Mill's *Logic* was designed to teach, it was
the notion of a science of social development, in which
there could be no breaks, no want of continuity in the
natural order.   A science of historical sociology could
not admit that, at a given period in the world's development, a character arose which had no relation to the
past, and no roots in the existing social conditions.   Yet
here in the last of Mill's writings there is the suggestion
that Christ was charged with "a special, express, and
unique commission from God to lead mankind to truth
and virtue."†   The passage in which these words occur
has often been quoted, but it is worth while to quote it
once more.   If it proves nothing else, it proves how
ready Mill was to find some sympathetic alliance with
those whose feelings he had so obviously outraged in the
earlier essays.   On the strength of this passage it has

* This consideration would, of course, only lead up to metem-
psychosis, not personal immortality.

† *Essays on Religion*, p. 255.

been suggested that Mill was at bottom a religious man. Such a notion is clearly in direct contradiction to the facts of his life. But he was, as we have had many opportunities of seeing, a man of uncommon warmth and intensity of feeling; and it is in the light rather of his emotional than of his religious character that the following words should be regarded :—

"Whatever else may be taken away from us by rational criticism, Christ is still left; a unique figure not more unlike all his precursors than all his followers, even those who had the direct benefit of his personal teaching. It is of no use to say that Christ, as exhibited in the Gospels, is not historical, and that we know not how much of what is admirable has been superadded by the tradition of his followers. The tradition of followers suffices to insert any number of marvels, but who among his disciples or among their proselytes was capable of inventing the sayings ascribed to Jesus, or of imagining the life and character revealed in the Gospels? . . . But about the life and sayings of Jesus there is a stamp of personal originality, combined with profundity of insight, which, if we abandon the idle expectation of finding scientific precision where something very different was aimed at, must place the Prophet of Nazareth, even in the estimation of those who have no belief in his inspiration, in the very first rank of the men of sublime genius of whom our species can boast. When this pre-eminent genius is combined with the qualities of probably the greatest moral reformer and martyr to that mission who ever existed upon earth, religion cannot be said to have made a bad choice in pitching upon this man as the ideal representative and guide of humanity; nor even now would it be easy, even for an unbeliever, to find a better translation of the rule of virtue from the abstract into the concrete than to endeavour so to live that Christ would approve our life. When to this we add that to the conception of the rational Sceptic it remains a possibility that Christ actually was what he supposed himself to be—not God, for he never made the smallest pretension to that character, and would probably have thought such a pretension as blasphemous, as it seemed to the men who condemned him—but a man, charged with a special, express, and unique commission from God to lead mankind to truth and virtue ; we may well conclude that the influences of religion on the character, which will remain after rational criticism has done its utmost against the evidences of religion, are well worth preserving, and that what they lack in direct strength as compared with those of a firmer belief, is more than compensated by the greater truth and rectitude of the morality they sanction."

This is a striking paragraph on many grounds, and perhaps it is no wonder that Mr. Morley, in reviewing the essay, should have felt that the Mill he knew and admired was slipping from his grasp.   But it need cause no wonder to those who accept that conception of Mill's character which it has been the object of these pages to enforce.   Let us remind ourselves that Mill had acknowledged as his chief office in the realm of thought to see the truth in the views of opponents, and to put the adversary's case, as was said of him in the House, better than the adversary himself could have put it.   The sentences in the *Autobiography* are quite decisive on this point :—" I thought myself much superior to most of my contemporaries in willingness and ability to learn from anybody ; as I found hardly anyone who made such a point of examining what was said in defence of all opinions, however new or however old, in the conviction that even if they were errors there might be a substratum of truth underneath them, and that, in any case, the discovery of what it was that made them plausible would be a benefit to truth." . . . " Goethe's device, ' many-sidedness,' was one which I would most willingly have taken for mine."* A man who takes such a view of his duties would be likely

Autobiography, pp. 163, 242, 243.

enough to astonish his more dogmatic and more logical friends.

In truth, Mill's character was eminently receptive of all the influences to which it was subjected. In his youth the prevailing influence is Bentham and James Mill; then comes the time when Sterling and Carlyle gain a large share of his sympathies; to that succeeds the influence of Mrs. Taylor; and after his wife's death, his views (as in the Essay on Theism, which was composed after his bereavement) seem to swing back on some of the older lines from which her ascendency over his mind had diverted them. It is his mental receptivity which constitutes, perhaps, his chief charm; it is that which explains his aims of reconciliation and mediatorship. But it is this also which gives that vacillation which here and there we have noticed in his grasp of doctrines, and leaves us with the final verdict that he belongs to a transitional period of thought. No one but a "transitional" thinker could, for instance, have written the following sentence in his Essay on Theism— "It is perfectly conceivable that religion may be morally useful without being intellectually sustainable." Such a phrase reminds us of the allegorical devices within which the less audacious spirits took refuge in their criticism of early mythology. It is like the Legal Fictions, which serve as a compromise for those who desire to retain the letter while they change the spirit of old institutions. But it is not written in the temper either of the clear-eyed iconoclast, or the constructive reformer. It belongs to the middle period between two eras, when men's thoughts are swaying ἐν μεταιχμίᾳ σκότου, in the battle-ground of darkness.

Enough, however, has already been said of Mill in this aspect. We have seen that he has a destructive side, and also a constructive side. As a destroyer, he works with Bentham and James Mill, and certainly, as Dr. Bain remarks, no more formidable trio can be imagined in the work of pulling down rotten institutions. As a constructor, he stands more isolated, for everywhere the ground has to be prepared for the newer edifices. We have certainly no desire to depreciate the value of his constructive agency. In providing science with a careful and elaborate theory of Induction, in sketching the outlines of a new science of Sociology, in discussing the dangers and the inevitableness of Democracy—in these and many other points his influence over the present generation can hardly be exaggerated. If we see, or think we see, further, it is because we stand on his shoulders. Nor is it possible to give an exhaustive enumeration of the various spheres in which his influence has been felt. No calculus, it has been well said, can integrate the innumerable little pulses of knowledge and of thought that he has made to vibrate in the minds of his generation. In logic, in ethics, in politics, we have nourished ourselves at his springs. Let us make the full acknowledgment of our debt, and also add that while all that is worst in him belongs to the eighteenth century, all that is best is akin to the highest, best spirit of the nineteenth.

In Mill's case, a longer study may perhaps lessen our admiration of him as a thinker, but increases our affection for him, as a man. Everything about him, it is true, is set in a quiet key. But perhaps the delicate spirit of self-effacement only adds to the power of the teacher. With his temper of sobriety and reserve, he did not think for men ; he rather made them think for themselves. Such, at least, is the opinion of Mr. Morley, who, on this point, is a competent judge.* Let us note, in passing, that he discovered Tennyson for his generation, that he saved Lord Durham by his quick insight into the value of his report, and that he rescued Carlyle's *French Revolution* from a too probable failure. If, in these matters, he guided the opinions of his countrymen, in other respects he held before them a splendid example of disinterested-ness, of courage, and of zeal for mankind. It required, probably, no little courage to face public opinion as he did on the question of the American War and of Governor Eyre. It certainly required no less disinterested-ness to write the articles on Bentham and Coleridge, and compose the Essay on Theism. And as to his love of his kind, there is abundant evidence. He cordially sympa-thised with every form of improvement, and did what-ever lay in him to aid the contrivers of new and beneficial schemes. " He was a strong supporter," says Dr. Bain, " of Mr. Chadwick's Poor-Law and Sanitary Legislation. He was quite exultant when the Peel Government of 1841 acquiesced in the Penny Postage, which Peel had at first opposed. His taking up of Hare's scheme of Representation was a notable illustra-tion of his readiness to embrace proposals that he had no hand in suggesting."† Even the Londoner, as he walks

---

* See " Death of Mr. Mill," *Fortnightly Review,* 1873.

† He was so uniformly courteous to opponents that it is a matter of surprise that he should have been discourteous enough to refuse to see the then Crown Princess of Prussia and the Princess Alice when they proposed to go to Avignon to visit him.

down Piccadilly, has occasion, though he probably does
not know it, to bless Mill's memory. When Lord Lincoln
(so Dr. Bain says) was Chief Commissioner of Woods and
Forests, Piccadilly was widened by taking a slice off the
Green Park. A row of trees was included in the addition,
and would, in all probability, have been cut down. Mill
intervened at the right moment, and induced Lord
Lincoln to preserve the row as they now remain at the
street-edge of the pavement. *

No pleasanter picture of Mill as a man can be found
than in the sympathetic pages which Mr. Morley wrote
in the *Fortnightly Review* on the occasion of his death.
Perhaps no more fitting way can be found of taking
leave of Mill than the reproduction of them here :—

"The last time I saw him was a few days before he left England.
He came to spend a day with me in the country, of which the
following rough notes happened to be written at the time in a letter
to a friend :—

" He came down by a morning train to G. Station, where I was
waiting for him. He was in his most even and mellow humour.
We walked in a leisurely way, and through roundabout tracks,
for some four hours along the ancient green road, which you know,
over the high grassy downs, into old chalk-pits picturesque with
juniper and yew, across heaths and commons, and so up to our
windy promontory, where the majestic prospect stirred him with
lively delight. You know he is a fervent botanist, and every ten
minutes he stooped to look at this or that on the path. Unluckily
I am ignorant of the very rudiments of the matter, so his
parenthetic enthusiasms were lost upon me.

"Of course he talked, and talked well. He admitted that
Goethe had added new points of view to life, but has a deep dislike
of his moral character ; wondered how a man who could draw the
sorrows of a deserted woman like Aurelia in *Wilhelm Meister*,
should yet have behaved so systematically ill to women. Goethe

* Bain : *J. S. Mill*, p. 154.

tried as hard as he could to be a Greek, yet his failure to produce anything perfect in form except a few lyrics proves the irresistible expansion of the modern spirit, and the inadequateness of the Greek type to the modern needs of activity and expression. Greatly prefers Schiller in all respects; turning to him from Goethe is like going into the fresh air from a hot-house. Spoke of style; thinks Goldsmith unsurpassed; then Addison comes. Greatly dislikes the style of Junius and of Gibbon; indeed, thinks meanly of the latter in all respects, except for his research, which alone of the work of that century stands the test of nineteenth century criticism. Did not agree with me that George Sand's is the high-water mark of prose, but yet could not name anybody higher, and admitted that her prose stirs you like music.

"Seemed disposed to think that the most feasible solution of the Irish University question is a Catholic University, the restrictive and obscurantist tendencies of which you may expect to have checked by the active competition of life with men trained in more enlightened systems. Spoke of Home Rule.

"Made remarks on the difference in the feeling of modern refusers of Christianity as compared with men like his father, impassioned deniers, who believed that if only you broke up the power of the priests and checked superstition, all would go well—a dream from which they were partially awakened by seeing that the French Revolution, which overthrew the Church, still did not bring the millennium. His radical friends used to be very angry with him for loving Wordsworth. 'Wordsworth,' I used to say, 'is against you, no doubt, in the battle which you are now waging, but after you have won, the world will need more than ever those qualities which Wordsworth is keeping alive and nourishing.'

"In his youth mere negation of religion was a firm bond of union, social and otherwise, between men who agreed in nothing else. . . . . And so forth, full of suggestiveness and interest all through. When he got here he chatted to R. over lunch with something of the amiableness of a child, about the wild flowers, the ways of insects, and notes of birds. He was impatient for the song of the nightingale. Then I drove him to our road-side station, and one of the most delightful days of my life came to its end, like all other days delightful and sorrowful."

12

When the news arrived of his death, it was said that a great spirit had gone. We may still repeat the words. Perhaps we seek to remember all that he did in the world. Perhaps our thoughts prefer to linger round those simple scenes of feeling and affection which were enacted amid the Fox family at Falmouth. But as Mill himself said, his work was done, and he could take leave of the world in the words of Socrates : " Wherefore let a man be of good cheer about his soul, who has cast away the pleasures and ornaments of the body as alien to him, and hurtful rather in their effects, and has followed after the pleasures of knowledge in this life ; who has arrayed the soul in her own proper jewels, which are temperance and justice and courage and nobility and truth. Thus adorned, she is ready to go on her journey to the world below, whenever her hour comes." *

* Plato : *Phædo,* 115.

INDEX.

GENEALOGY OF THE MILL FAMILY.

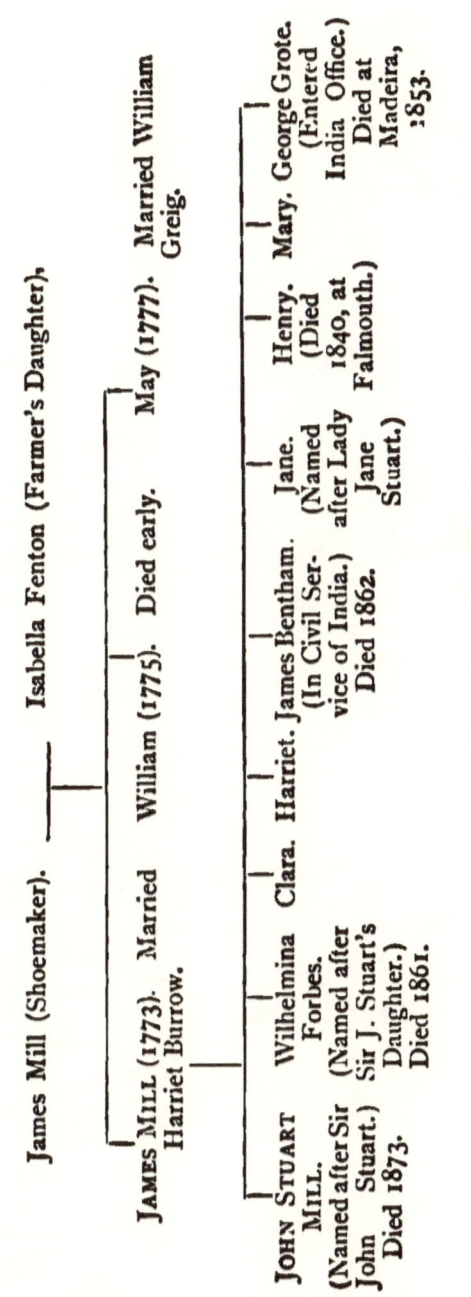

James Mill (Shoemaker). ——— Isabella Fenton (Farmer's Daughter).

JAMES MILL (1773). Married Harriet Burrow.   William (1775). Died early.   May (1777). Married William Greig.

JOHN STUART MILL. (Named after Sir John Stuart.) Died 1873.

Wilhelmina Forbes. (Named after Sir J. Stuart's Daughter.) Died 1861.

Clara.   Harriet.   James Bentham. (In Civil Service of India.) Died 1862.   Jane. (Named after Lady Jane Stuart.)   Henry. (Died 1840, at Falmouth.)   Mary. George Grote. (Entered India Office.) Died at Madeira, 1853.

"The united careers of the two Mills covered exactly a century. A day chosen between the 23rd of April and the 7th of May 1973 would serve as a double centenary."—Bain: *J. S. Mill,* 195.

APPENDIX II.

CALENDAR

OF THE LIVES OF THE TWO MILLS.

JAMES MILL. (1773-1836.)	JOHN STUART MILL. (1806-1873.)
1773. James Mill born (April 6th). (Montrose Academy. Acquaintance with Sir John Stuart of Fettercairn.)	
1790. Goes to the University of Edinburgh at seventeen and a half. "Brought forward" for the ministry. Educates Wilhelmina, daughter of Sir J. Stuart.	
1798. Licensed as preacher.	
1802. Goes to London with Sir John Stuart. Writes in the *Anti-Jacobite Review* and *Literary Journal.*	
1804. A volunteer.	
1805. Editor of *St. James' Chronicle.* Marries Harriet Burrow.	
1806. Begins *History of India.* John Stuart born.	1806. J. S. Mill born, May 20th. (Early education with father up to 1820.)
1808. Begins to write for the *Edinburgh Review.*	
—— Intimacy begun with Bentham.	
1809. *Miranda and Spanish America* —article in *Edinburgh Review.*	
1811. Introduction to Ricardo and Place.	
1812. Anxiety for John's training (in case of his own death).	
1813. Summer tour with John and Bentham.	

JAMES MILL.

1817. Publication of *History of India.*
1819. Appointment at India House.
1820. Article on *Government.*

1821. *Elements of Political Economy.*

1822. Begins *Analysis of Human Mind.* (Published 1829.)

1823 Appointed First Assistant Examiner at the India House.

1824. In *Westminster Review* criticises the *Edinburgh Review.* The *Quarterly* also overhauled.
1825. Southey's *Book of the Church* attacked in *Westminster Review.* Founding of the University of London.

1826. *Ecclesiastical Establishments*—article in *Westminster Review.*
1827. Article in *Parliamentary History and Review.*

1829. *Analysis of Human Mind* published. Macaulay's attack on *Government*—article in the *Edinburgh Review.*

1830. Culmination of Mill's career. India Charter renewal. Mill made Head Examiner.

1832. "Agony Week" of Reform Movement. Death of Bentham (June 6).

JOHN STUART MILL.

1820. } In France with Sir Samuel
1821. } Bentham.
1821. Begins Psychological studies (Condillac).
1822. Reads History of French Revolution. Studies Law with Austin. Dumont on Bentham read and admired. Studies in English philosophy. Writes in the *Traveller.*
1823. Utilitarian Society. Letters to *Morning Chronicle* on Richard Carlile prosecutions. Enters India House as clerk.
1824. Contributes to *Westminster Review* in continuation of father's attack on *Edinburgh Review.*
1825. Edits Bentham's book on Evidence. Starting of *Parliamentary History and Review.* Learns German. Founding of Speculative Debating Society. Writes in the *Westminster Review.*

1827. Readings at Grote's house on Logic. Article, *Whately's Logic* written for *Westminster Review* (published January 1828).
1828. Acquaintance with Maurice and Sterling. Reads Wordsworth for the first time. Made Assistant Examiner in India House.
1829. Change in his views on Logic of Politics, owing to Macaulay's attack on Father. Readings at Grote's house on *Analysis of Human Mind.*
1830. Puts on paper ideas on Logical Distinctions and Import of Propositions. First acquaintance with French Philosophy of History (St. Simonians and Comte). Goes to Paris. Writes in *Examiner* on French Politics. *Prospects in France.*
1831. *Essays on Unsettled Questions in Political Economy* written (only published 1844). Resumes Study of Logical Axioms and Theory of Syllogism. First introduction to Mrs. Taylor.
1832. Essays in *Tait's Magazine* and *Jurist.*
1833. *Thoughts on Poetry (Monthly Repository).*

JAMES MILL.

1835. *State of the Nation*, in *London Review*. *Church and its Reform*, in *London Review*. Attack of hæmorrhage. *Fragment on Mackintosh*. *Land Reform*, in *London Review*.

1836. *Aristocracy*, in *London Review*. Dialogue, *Whether Political Economy is useful*, in *London Review*. (Mill's last work.) Death of James Mill (June 23).

JOHN STUART MILL.

1835. Reads De Tocqueville's *Democracy in America*. *London Review* article on Sedgwick.

1836. Father's death. Illness and three months' absence in Switzerland and Italy. *London and Westminster Review* article on Civilisation. Promoted to second Assistant (£800) and first Assistant (£1200).

1837. *Canada and Lord Durham*, article written for *London and Westminster Review*. Also article on Carlyle's *French Revolution*.

1838. *Bentham*, article in *London and Westminster Review*. Finishes third book of his *Logic*.

1839. Illness. Six months' absence in Italy.

1840. *Coleridge*, article in *London and Westminster Review*. First contribution to *Edinburgh Review* on De Tocqueville. Writes sixth book of his *Logic*. With brother Henry and the Fox family at Falmouth.

1841-6. Correspondence with Comte.

1842. Review of Bailey's *Theory of Vision* in the *Westminster Review*. Loss of money, owing to American repudiation.

1843. *System of Logic* published.

1844. *Michelet*, in *Edinburgh Review*.

1845. *Claims of Labour* and *Guizot*, in *Edinburgh Review*.

1846. Review of Grote's *Greece* (vols. i. and ii.) in *Edinburgh Review*.

1847. Articles on *Irish Affairs* in the *Chronicle*.

1848. *Political Economy* published. Accident, owing to a fall, and illness.

1849. Vindication of French Revolution of 1848, in reply to Lord Brougham in *Westminster Review*.

1851. Marriage with Mrs. Taylor.

1852. Article on Whewell's *Moral Philosophy* in *Westminster Review*.

1853. Final article on Grote's *Greece* in *Edinburgh Review*.

1854. Serious illness, and consequent tour in Sicily, Italy, and Greece for eight months.

JOHN STUART MILL.

1856. Head of Examiners' Office in the India House.

1857. Drafts petition to Parliament on behalf of East India Company threatened with extinction.

1858. Official work over, owing to transfer of India to the Crown. Death of Wife.

1859. *Liberty* and *Thoughts on Parliamentary Reform* published.

1861. *Representative Government* published.

1862. Writes in *Fraser* on American Civil War, taking the side of the North. Also on same subject in *Westminster Review*. Tour in Greece and Asia Minor.

1863. *Utilitarianism* published. Article on John Austin in *Edinburgh Review.*

1864. Articles on *Comte and Positivism.*

1865. *Examination of Sir W. Hamilton* published. Election at Westminster.

1866. Article on Grote's *Plato.*

1867. Address to students of St. Andrews as Rector.

1868. Pamphlet on *England and Ireland.* Defeated at Westminster in General Election by W. H. Smith. Retires to Avignon.

1869. Edition of father's *Analysis of Human Mind* published. *Subjection of Women* published. *Endowments* and *Labour and its Claims* (a review of Thornton's book). Meditates writing a book on Socialism.

1871. Attends Grote's funeral in Westminster Abbey.

1873. Death (May 8).
In the three last years of his life worked at Land Question.
Posthumous works :—
Autobiography, 1873.
Three essays on Religion. } 1874.
Chapters on Socialism. } *Fortnightly Review,* 1879.

BIBLIOGRAPHY.

BY

JOHN P. ANDERSON

(British Museum).

I. WORKS.

Dissertations and Discussions; political, philosophical, and historical. Reprinted chiefly from the *Edinburgh* and *Westminster Reviews.* 4 vols. London, 1859-75, 8vo.
——Second edition. 4 vols. London, 1875, 8vo.

Auguste Comte and Positivism. Reprinted from the *Westminster Review.* London, 1865, 8vo.
——Second edition. London, 1866, 8vo.
——Third edition. London, 1882, 8vo.
Vol. xvi. of *The English and Foreign Philosophical Library.*

Autobiography. [Edited by Helen Taylor.] London, 1873, 8vo.
——Another edition. New York, 1874, 8vo.

Considerations on Representative Government. London, 1861, 8vo.
——Second edition. London, 1861, 8vo.
——Third edition. London, 1865, 8vo.

England and Ireland. London, 1868, 8vo.

Essays on some unsettled questions of Political Economy. London, 1844, 8vo.
These Essays were written in 1830-31.
——Second edition. London, 1874, 8vo.

An examination of Sir W. Hamilton's Philosophy, and of the principal Philosophical questions discussed in his writings. London, 1865, 8vo.
——Second edition. London, 1865, 8vo.
——Third edition. London, 1867, 8vo.
——Fifth edition. London, 1878, 8vo.
Memorandum of the Improvements in the Administration of India during the last thirty years, and the petition of the East-India Company to Parliament [drawn up by John Stuart Mill]. London, 1858, 8vo.
Nature, the Utility of Religion and Theism. [With introductory notice by Helen Taylor.] London, 1874, 8vo.
——Second edition. London, 1874, 8vo.
On Liberty. London, 1859, 8vo.
——Third edition. London, 1864, 8vo.
Principles of Political Economy, with some of their applications to Social Philosophy. 2 vols. London, 1848, 8vo.
——Second edition. 2 vols. London, 1849, 8vo.
——Third edition. 2 vols. London, 1852, 8vo.
——Fourth edition. 2 vols. London, 1857, 8vo.
——Fifth edition. 2 vols. London, 1862, 8vo.
——Sixth edition. 2 vols. London, 1865, 8vo.
—— ——Abridged, with notes, and a Sketch of the History of Political Economy, by J. L. Laughlin, etc. New York, 1884, 8vo.

Principles of Political Economy, Chapters and Speeches on the Irish Land Question. Reprinted from *Principles of Political Economy* and *Hansard's Debates.* London, 1870, 8vo.
The Subjection of Women. London, 1869, 8vo.
——Second edition. London, 1869, 8vo.
——Fourth edition. London, 1878, 8vo.
A System of Logic, ratiocination and induction, being a connected view of the principles of evidence and the methods of scientific investigation. 2 vols. London, 1843, 8vo.
——Third edition. 2 vols. London, 1851, 8vo.
——Fourth edition. 2 vols. London, 1856, 8vo.
——Fifth edition. 2 vols. London, 1862, 8vo.
——Seventh edition. 2 vols. London, 1868, 8vo.
——Eighth edition. London, 1872, 8vo.
——Ninth edition. 2 vols. London, 1875, 8vo.
——People's edition. London, 1884, 8vo.
—— ——Analysis of Mr. Mill's System of Logic. By W. Stebbing. London, 1864, 12mo.
—— ——The Student's Handbook, synoptical and explanatory of J. S. Mill's System of Logic. By A. H. Killick. London, 1870, 8vo.
Thoughts on Parliamentary Reform. London, 1859, 8vo.
——Second edition, with additions. London, 1859, 8vo.

Utilitarianism. Reprinted from *Fraser's Magazine.* London, 1863, 8vo.
——Second edition. London, 1864, 8vo.
——Another edition. London, 1871, 8vo.

II. MISCELLANEOUS.

Analysis of the Phenomena of the Human Mind. By James Mill. A new edition, with notes illustrative and critical, by A. Bain, A. Findlater, and G. Grote. Edited, with additional notes, by John Stuart Mill. 2 vols. London, 1869, 8vo.

Inaugural Address delivered to the University of St. Andrew's, February 1st, 1867. London, 1867, 8vo.

The *London Review,* afterwards incorporated into the *Westminster Review,* under the title of the *London and Westminster Review.* [Edited by J. S. Mill]. London, 1834-40, 8vo.

Memories of Old Friends ; being extracts from the journals and letters of Caroline Fox, from 1835 to 1871. Edited by H. N. Pym. Second edition. To which are added fourteen original letters from J. S. Mill, etc. 2 vols. London, 1882, 8vo.

Programme of the Land Tenure Reform Association, with an explanatory statement by J. S. Mill. London, 1871, 8vo,

Public Responsibility and Vote by Ballot. By Henry Romilly. To which are appended, a letter from J. S. Mill to the Editor of the *Reader,* 29th April, 1865, and observations thereon. London, 1867, 8vo.

Rationale of judicial evidence, specially applied to English practice. From the manuscripts of Jeremy Bentham. 5 vols. [Edited by J. Stuart Mill]. London, 1827, 8vo.

Selection from the Correspondence of the late Macvey Napier, Esq. London, 1879, 8vo.
Contains several letters from J. S. Mill.

Speech in favour of Women's Suffrage. January 12th, 1871. Edinburgh, 1873, 8vo.

Speech on the Admission of Women to the Electoral Franchise. Spoken in the House of Commons, May 20th, 1867. London, 1867, 8vo.

Views of J. S. Mill on England's danger through the suppression of her maritime power. London, 1874, 8vo.
Consists of a letter from J. S. Mill, and his Speech in the House of Commons, August 5, 1867.

III. APPENDIX.

BIOGRAPHY, CRITICISM, ETC.

Alexander, Patrick P.—Mill and Carlyle. An examination of J. Stuart Mill's Doctrine of Causation in relation to moral freedom, etc. Edinburgh, 1866, 8vo.
——Moral Causation ; or notes on Mr. Mill's Notes to the Chapter on "Freedom," in the third edition of his " Examination of Sir W. Hamilton's Philosophy." Edinburgh, 1868, 8vo.

Alexander, Patrick P.—Second edition, revised and extended. Edinburgh and London, 1875, 8vo.

Antichrist.—The Jesus Christ of John Stuart Mill. By Antichrist. London, 1875, 8vo.

B., H. R. F., *i.e.*, H. R. Fox Bourne.—John Stuart Mill; notices of his life and works. Together with two papers written by him on the Land Question. [Edited by H. R. F. B.] Reprinted from the *Examiner.* London, 1873, 8vo.

Bain, Alexander.—John Stuart Mill. A Criticism ; with personal recollections. London, Aberdeen [printed], 1882, 8vo.

Ballantyne, J. R.—On the Philosophy of Induction. [Compiled by J. R. Ballantyne, principally from J. S. Mill's System of Logic.] Allahabad, 1851 ? 8vo.

Beggs, Thomas.—The Deterrent Influence of Capital Punishment. Being a reply to the Speech of J. Stuart Mill, delivered in the House of Commons on the 21st of April 1868. London, 1868, 8vo.
——Second edition. London, 1868, 8vo.

Birks, Thomas Rawson.—Modern Utilitarianism, or the Systems of Paley, Bentham, and Mill examined and compared. London, Cambridge [printed], 1874, 8vo.

Blackwood, F. T. H., *Earl of Dufferin.*—Mr. Mill's Plan for the Pacification of Ireland examined. London, 1868, 8vo.
——Another edition. London, 1868, 8vo.

Brandes, Dr. Georg.—Eminent Authors of the Nineteenth Century. Literary Portraits. Translated from the original by R. B. Anderson. New York, 1886, 8vo.
John Stuart Mill, pp. 123-146.

Bridges, John Henry.—The Unity of Comte's Life and Doctrine. A reply to strictures on Comte's later writings, addressed to J. S. Mill. London [Bungay, printed], 1866, 8vo.

Browne, Walter R.—The Autobiography of J. S. Mill. London, 1874, 8vo.
——Christian Evidence Lectures. Strivings for the Faith, etc. London, 1874, 8vo.
The Autobiography of John Stuart Mill. By W. R. Browne, pp. 259-287.

Cannegieter, Dr. T.—De Nuttigheidsleer van John Stuart Mill en Professor Van der Wijck. Groningen, 1876, 8vo.

Carlyle Thomas.—Reminiscences. Edited by C. E. Norton. 2 vols. London, 1887, 8vo.
References to J. S. Mill.

Christie, W. D.—J. S. Mill and Mr. A. Hayward. A reply about Mill to a letter [from A. Hayward] to the Rev. Stopford Brooke, privately circulated and actually published. London, 1873, 8vo.

Comte, J. A. M. F. X.—Lettrés à J. S. Mill, 1841-1846. Paris, 1877, 8vo.

Conway, Moncure Daniel. — In Memoriam. A Memorial Discourse in honour of John Stuart Mill, May 25th, 1873. [London, 1873], 16mo.

Courtney, William L.—The Metaphysics of J. S. Mill. London, 1879, 8vo.

Deuchar, Robert. — Review of "An Examination of the Hamiltonian Philosophy, by J. S. Mill," etc. Edinburgh, 1865, 8vo.

Eccarius, J. Georg. — Eines Arbeiters Widerlegung der national-ökonomischen Lehren J. S. Mill's. Berlin, Leipzig [printed], 1869, 8vo.

English, William Watson. — An Essay on Moral Philosophy . . . with a few Criticisms . . . of Professor Tyndall, the Duke of Argyll, and J. S. Mill. London, 1869, 8vo.

Examiner. — See supra, B., H. R. F.

Froude, James Anthony. — Thomas Carlyle, a history of the first forty years of his life etc. 2 vols. London, 1882, 8vo.
  Numerous references to J. S. Mill.

——Thomas Carlyle, a history of his life in London, etc. 2 vols. London, 1884, 8vo.
  Numerous references to J. S. Mill.

Galasso, Antonio. — Della conciliazione dell'egoismo coll' altruismo - secondo J. S. Mill. Discorso, etc. [Estratto dal vol. xviii. degli "Atti del'Accademia di Scienze morali e politiche."] Napoli, 1883, 8vo.

Gneist, Heinrich Rudolph. — Gneist und Stuart Mill. Alt-Englische und Neu-Englische Staatsanschaung. Eine politische Parallele. Berlin, 1869, 8vo.

Goggia, P. E. — La Mente di Mill. Saggio di logica positiva applicata specialmente alla storia. Livorno, 1869, 8vo.

Grant, Sir Alexander, Bart. — Recess Studies. Edinburgh, 1870, 8vo.
  Mr. Mill on Trades Unions. A Criticism. By James Stirling, pp. 309-332.

Grote, George. — Review of the Work of Mr. J. S. Mill, entitled "Examination of Sir W. Hamilton's Philosophy." [Reprinted from the *Westminster Review.*] London, 1868 [1867], 8vo.

Grote, John. — An examination of the Utilitarian Philosophy [of J. S. Mill.] Edited by J. B. Mayor. Cambridge, 1870, 8vo.

——The Minor Works of G. Grote. London, 1873, 8vo.
  Review of John Stuart Mill on the Philosophy of Sir William Hamilton, pp. 277-330; reprinted from the *Westminster Review*, 1866.

Hazard, Rowland G. — Two Letters on Causation and Freedom in Willing, addressed to J. S. Mill [in reference to his philosophical work]. Boston, 1869, 8vo.

Hodgson, Shadworth H. — Outcast Essays and Verse Translations. London, 1881, 8vo.
  De Quincey as Political Economist, or De Quincey and Mill on Supply and Demand, pp. 67-98.

Holyoake, George Jacob. — A new Defence of the Ballot in consequence of Mr. Mill's objections to it. London, 1868, 8vo.

Index, *pseud* [*i.e.* George Vasey]. — Individual Liberty, moral and licentious; in which the political fallacies of J. S. Mill's Essay "On Liberty" are pointed out. By Index. London, 1867, 8vo.

——Second edition. London, 1877, 8vo.

Inquirer.—The Battle of the two Philosophers [Sir W. Hamilton, Bart., and J. S. Mill]. By an Inquirer. London, 1866, 12mo.

Kohn, Benno.—Untersuchungen über das Causal Problem auf dem Boden einer Kritik der einschlägigen Lehren J. S. Mills. Wien, 1881, 8vo.

Lange, Friedrich A.—J. S. Mill's Ansichten über die sociale Frage und die angebliche Umwälzung der Social-wissenschaft durch Carey. Dinsburg, 1866, 8vo.

Levin, Thomas W.—Notes on Inductive Logic, Book I; being an introduction to Mill's System of Logic. Cambridge, 1885, 16mo.

Liberal.—A Review of Mr. J. S. Mill's Essay "On Liberty;" and an investigation of his claim to be considered the leading Philosopher and Thinker of the Age. Also a refutation of his two statements:—I. That Christian Morality teaches us to be selfish. II. That the working-classes of this country are mostly habitual liars. By a Liberal. London, 1867, 8vo.

Littré, M. P. E.—Auguste Comte et Stuart Mill. [An answer to a work of the latter, entitled, "Auguste Comte and Positivism."] Suivi de Stuart Mill et la Philosophie Positive par G. Wyrouboff [on the same subject]. London [1866], 8vo.

Löchen, Arne.—Om J. Stuart Mill's Logik. En kritisk studie. Kristiania, 1885, 8vo.

Longe, Francis D.—A refutation of the wage-fund theory of modern Political Economy as enunciated by Mr. Mill and Mr. Fawcett. London, 1866, 8vo.

——A Critical Examination of Mr. George's "Progress and Poverty," and Mr. Mill's "Theory of Wages." London [1883], 8vo.

Lyall, A.—Agonistes; or Philosophical Strictures, etc. London, 1856, 8vo.
    Mill's "System of Logic," pp. 307-385.

MacCall, William.—The Newest Materialism; sundry papers on the books of Mill, Comte, etc. London, 1873, 8vo.

MacCosh, James.—An Examination of J. S. Mill's Philosophy, being a defence of fundamental truth. London, 1866, 8vo.

——Second edition, with additions. London, 1877, 8vo.

——Philosophical Papers. I. Examination of Sir W. Hamilton's Logic. II. Reply to Mr. Mill's third edition. III. Present state of moral philosophy in Britain. London, 1868, 8vo.

Manning, H. E., *Cardinal.*—Essays on Religion and Literature by various writers. Edited by Henry Edward, Archbishop of Westminster. London, 1874, 8vo.
    Mr. Mill on Liberty of the Press, by Edward Lucas. Third series, pp. 142-173.

Mansel, Henry Longueville.—The Philosophy of the Conditional; comprising some remarks on Sir W. Hamilton's Philosophy, and on Mr. J. S. Mill's Examination of that Philosophy. (Reprinted, with additions, from "The Contemporary Review.") London, 1866, 8vo.

Marston, Mansfield.—The Life of J. S. Mill, etc. London [1873], 8vo.

Martineau, James.—Essays philosophical and theological. New York, 1879, 8vo.
    John Stuart Mill, vol 1., pp. 6-120.

Masson, David.—Recent British Philosophy: a review, with criticisms; including some comments on Mr. Mill's answer to Sir W. Hamilton. London, 1865, 8vo.

——Second edition. London, 1867, 8vo.

——Third edition, with an additional chapter. London, 1877, 8vo.

Mill, John Stuart.—Objections to the Ballot, answered from the writings and speeches of Mill, Grote, etc. London, 1837, 8vo.

——Who is the "Reformer," J. S. Mill or John Bright? London, 1859, 8vo.

——Utilitarianism explained and exemplified in moral and political government. [Being a reply to J. S. Mill's work, entitled "Utilitarianism."] London, 1864, 8vo.

——Hamilton *versus* Mill. A thorough discussion of each chapter in Mr. John S. Mill's Examination of Hamilton's Logic and Philosophy, etc Edinburgh, 1866, 8vo.

——Odd Bricks from a tumbledown private building. [Being remarks on J. S. Mill's work, entitled "An Examination of Sir W. Hamilton's Philosophy," etc.] By a retired Constructor. London, 1866, 12mo.

——Mr. J. S. Mill and the Ballot: a criticism of his opinions as expressed in "Thoughts on Parliamentary Reform." By a Westminster Elector. London, 1869, 8vo.

——The Grosvenor Papers. An Answer to Mr. J. Stuart Mill's "Subjection of Women." London, 1869, 8vo.

——A Reply to John Stuart Mill on the Subjection of Women. Philadelphia, 1870, 8vo.

——Leaving us an Example: is it living—and why? An Enquiry suggested by certain passages in J. S. Mill's "Essays on Religion." London [1876], 8vo.

Millet, J.—An Millius veram Mathematicorum axiomatum originem invenerit, etc. Parisiis, 1867, 8vo.

Minto, Professor.—John Stuart Mill. (In the *Encyclopædia Britannica*, vol. xvi.) Edinburgh, 1883, 4to.

Morley, John. — Critical Miscellanies. Second series. London, 1877, 8vo.
    The death of Mr. Mill, Ser. ii., pp. 239-250; Mr. Mill's Autobiography, pp. 253-284; Mr. Mill on Religion, pp. 287-336.

N., N.—Thirteen pages on intellectual property, written with special reference to a doubtful doctrine of J. S. Mill, by one of his pupils (N. N.). Manchester [1876], 8vo.

Napier, Rt. Hon. Sir Joseph.—The Miracles. Butler's Argument on Miracles, explained and defended; with observations on Hume, Baden Powell, and J. S. Mill, etc. Dublin, 1863, 8vo.

Neaves, Lord.—Stuart Mill on Mind and Matter. (In verse.) *Blackwood's Edinburgh Magazine*, vol. 99, 1866, pp. 257-259, and vol. 100, pp. 245, 246.

Notes and Queries.—General Index to Notes and Queries. Five Series. London, 1856-1880, 4to.
Numerous references to Mill.

O'Hanlon, Hugh F.—A Criticism on J. S. Mill's Pure Idealism; and an attempt to show that, if logically carried out, it is pure Nihilism. Oxford [printed], London, 1866, 8vo.

Parker, Joseph.—J. S. Mill on Liberty. A Critique. London, 1865, 8vo.

Purnell, Thomas.—Literature and its Professors. London, 1867, 8vo.
John Stuart Mill, pp. 47-62.

Reybaud, Louis. — Economistes Modernes. Paris, 1862, 8vo.
John Stuart Mill, pp. 244-304.

Ribot, Th. — La Psychologie Anglaise Contemporaine. Paris, 1870, 8vo.
J. Stuart Mill, pp 87-144.

——English Psychology. Translated from the French of Th. Ribot. London, 1873, 8vo.
John Stuart Mill, pp. 78-123.

Sangar, James Mortimer.—Episcopal Vows. What do they mean? A letter to the Lord Bishop of St. David's on his recent endorsements of the alleged infidelity of J. S. Mill. London (1866), 8vo.

Scherer, Edmond.—Études Critiques sur la Littérature Contemporaine. Paris, 1863, 8vo.
John Stuart Mill (Representative Government), tom. i., pp. 299-320; reprinted from the *Temps.*

Schiel, J.—Die Methode der inductiven Forschung als die Methode der Naturforschung in gedrängter Darstellung hauptsächlich nach John Stuart Mill. Braunschweig, 1865, 8vo.

Seccombe, John Thomas.—Science, theism, and revelation, considered in relation to Mr. Mill's essays on nature, religion, and theism. London, King's Lynn (printed), 1875, 8vo.

Taine, Hippolyte A.—Le Positivisme Anglais, étude sur Stuart Mill. Paris, 1864, 12mo.

——English Positivism. A study on J. S. Mill. Translated by T. D. Haye. London, 1870, 8vo.

——Histoire de la Littérature Anglaise. 4 tom. Paris, 1863-4, 8vo.
La Philosophie, Stuart Mill, tom. iv., pp. 339-429.

——History of English Literature. 4 vols. London, 1873-4, 8vo.
Philosophy, Stuart Mill, vol. iv., pp. 357-426.

Taylor, Sir Henry.—Autobiography of Henry Taylor. 2 vols. London, 1885, 8vo.
References to J. S. Mill.

Thompson, Thomas Perronet.— The true theory of rent in opposition to Mr. Ricardo and others. Being an exposition of fallacies on rent, tithes, etc., in the form of a review of Mr. Mill's Elements of Political Economy. Ninth edition. London, 1832, 8vo.

Torrens, Robert.—The principles and practical operation of Sir R. Peel's Act of 1844 explained . . . and a critical examination of the chapter " On the regulation of a convertible Paper

Currency" in J. S. Mill's "Principles of Political Economy." London, 1857, 8vo.

Torens, Robert.—Another edition. London, 1858, 8vo.

——The Budget. . . . With an introduction, in which the Deduction Method, as presented in Mr. Mill's "System of Logic," is applied to the solution of some controverted questions in Political Economy. London, 1844, 8vo.

Whewell, William.—Of Induction, with especial reference to Mr. J. Stuart Mill's "System of Logic." London, Cambridge [printed], 1849, 16mo.

White, Carlos.— Ecce Femina : an attempt to solve the Woman Question. Being an examination of arguments in favor of female suffage by John Stuart Mill and others, etc. Hanover, N.H., 1870, 8vo.

MAGAZINE ARTICLES.

National Review, by J. Martineau, vol. 9, 1859, pp. 474-508.— Boston Review, by J. H. Ward, vol. 6, 1866, pp. 104-120.— Eclectic Magazine (with portrait), vol. 4 N.S., 1866, pp. 120-122.—Galaxy, by J. McCarthy, vol. 7, 1869, pp. 373-382.—Appleton's Journal of Literature (with portrait), vol. 3, 1870, pp. 126-129.—Quarterly Review, vol. 135, 1873, pp. 178-201. — Fraser's Magazine, vol. 8 N.S., 1873, pp. 663-681. — Macmillan's Magazine (Poem), by J. J. Murphy, vol. 28, 1873, pp. 348, 349.— Nation, by E. L. Godkin and

Mill, John Stuart.
C. Wright, vol. 16, 1873, pp. 350, 351, 382, 383.—Popular Science Monthly, by H. R. Fox-Bourne, H. Spencer, and others, vol. 3, 1873, pp. 367-388.—Nature, vol. 8, 1873, p. 47.—Canadian Monthly, by N. F. Davin, vol. 3, 1873, pp. 512-519.—La Renaissance, by E. Blémont, vol. 2, 1873, pp. 121-122.—International Review, by N. Porter, vol. 1, 1874, pp. 385-406.— Old and New, by E. E. Hale, vol. 9, 1874, pp. 128-135.— Contemporary Review, by Lord Blachford, vol. 28, 1876, pp. 508-536.— New Englander, by L. Adams, vol. 36, 1877, pp. 92-114, 425-444, 740-784.—Western, by Ellen M. Mitchell, vol. 3, 1877, pp. 555-561.—Mind, by A. Bain, vol. 4, 1879, pp. 211-229, 375-394, 520-541. — Popular Science Review, by A. Bain, vol. 14, 1879, pp. 697-714 ; vol. 15, pp. 327-345, 750-759 ; vol. 16, pp. 25-35, 501-507.

——and Christianity. Baptist Quarterly, by C. B. Crane, vol. 8, 1874, pp. 348-362.

——and Fundamental Truth, McCosh on. Princeton Review, by L. H. Atwater, vol. 38, 1866, pp. 416-424.

——and Goethe ; a Contrast. Westminster Review, vol. 46 N.S., 1874, pp. 38-70.

——and Inductive Origin of First Principles. Journal of Sacred Literature, vol. 9, 4th Series, 1866, pp. 1-35.

——Autobiography. St. Paul's, by H. Holbeach, vol. 13, 1873, pp. 686-701.—Victoria Magazine, vol. 22, 1873, pp. 181-189.—

Mill, John Stuart.
Revue des Deux Mondes, by
Auguste Laugel, tom. 108,
1873, pp. 906-937.—Quarterly
Review, vol. 136, 1874, pp.
150-179 ; same article, Littell's
Living Age, vol. 120, pp. 771-
787.—Westminster Review, vol.
45 N.S., 1874, pp. 122-159.—
Edinburgh Review, vol. 139,
1874, pp. 91-129.—Fortnightly
Review, by J. Morley, vol. 15
N.S., 1874, pp. 1-20—Contem-
porary Review, by J. M. Capes,
vol. 23, 1874, pp. .53-65.—
British Quarterly Review, vol.
59, 1874, pp. 195-215.—
Christian Observer, vol. 74,
1874, pp. 37-50. — Scribner's
Monthly, vol. 7, 1874, pp. 600-
611.—New Englander, by A. L.
Chapin, vol. 33, 1874, pp. 605-
622.—Catholic World, by J. L.
Spalding, vol. 18, 1874, pp.
721-733. — Nation, by A. V.
Dicey, vol. 18, 1874, pp. 26-28,
43, 44.—Galaxy, by R. G.
White, vol. 17, 1874, pp. 332-
343.—Baptist Quarterly, by H.
Lincoln, vol. 8, 1874, pp. 233-
250.—Eclectic Magazine (from
the Saturday Review), vol. 19
N.S., 1874, pp. 55-59.
——and the Destruction of Theism.
Princeton Review, by D. S.
Gregory, Sept. 1878, pp. 409-
448.
——Death of. Fortnightly Review, by J. Morley, vol. 19
N.S., 1873, pp. 669-676; same
article, Eclectic Magazine, vol.
18 N.S., pp. 207-212, and
Littell's Living Age, vol. 118,
pp. 159-164.
——Denial of Freewill. Dublin
Review, vol. 22 N.S., 1874,
pp. 326-361.

Mill, John Stuart.
——Denial of Necessary Truth.
Dublin Review, vol. 17 N.S.,
1871, pp. 285-318.
——Education and Science.—
Popular Science Monthly, vol.
4, 1874, pp. 368-373.
——Essay on Nature. Month, by
J. Rickaby, vol. 23, 1875, pp.
50-65.
——Essays on Religion. West-
minster Review, vol. 47 N.S.,
1875, pp. 1-28. — Fortnightly
Review, by J. Morley, vol. 16
N.S., pp. 634-651, and vol. 17,
1875, pp. 103-131.—Theological
Review, by C. B. Upton, vol.
12, 1875, pp. 127-145, 249-272.
——Examination of Hamilton's
Philosophy. Fortnightly Review,
by H. Spencer, vol. 1, 1865, pp.
531-550.—Bibliotheca Sacra, by
J. Haven, vol. 25, 1868, pp.
501-535.—Christian Examiner,
by O. B. Frothingham, vol 79,
1865, pp 301-327.—Dublin
Review, vol. 21 N.S., 1873,
pp. 1-49.
——Experimental Methods of,
Jevons on. Mind, by R. Adam-
son, vol. 3, 1878, pp. 415-417.
——for Westminster. Mac-
millan's Magazine, vol. 12,
1865, pp. 92-96.
——Fundamental Propositions.
Contemporary Review, by
Anthony Musgrave, vol. 24,
1874, pp. 728-749.
——Hayward on. Dublin Uni-
versity Magazine, vol. 82, 1873,
pp. 253-255.
——Influence of Writings of.
Contemporary Review, by Edith
Simcox, vol. 22, 1873, pp. 297-
317.
——Logic. British Critic, vol.
34, 1843, pp. 349-427.—Demo-

Mill, John Stuart.
cratic Review, vol. 15 N.S., 1844, pp. 441-453.—Revue des Deux Mondes, by H. Taine, tom. 32, 1861, pp. 44-82.

——*Metaphysics of, Courtney on.* Mind, by G. C. Robertson, vol. 4, 1879, pp. 421-426.

——*on Causation.* Dublin Review, vol. 27 N.S., 1876, pp. 57-82.

——*on the Foundation of Morality.* Dublin Review, vol. 18 N.S., 1872, pp. 44-76.

——*on Socialism.* To-Day, by Sydney Olivier, vol. 2 N.S., 1884, pp. 490-504.

——*on the Utility of Religion.* Month, by J. Rickaby, vol. 4, 3rd Series, 1875, pp. 393-408; vol. 5, pp. 169-180.

——*Philosophical Position of.* Dublin Review, vol. 22 N.S., 1874, pp. 1-38.

——*Philosophy of Necessary Truth and Causation.* New Englander, vol. 8, 1850, pp. 161-186.

——*Philosophy tested.* Contemporary Review, by W. S. Jevons, vol. 31, 1878, pp. 167-182, 256-275; vol. 32, pp. 88-99.—Mind, by G. C. Robertson, A. Strachey, and W. S. Jevons, vol. 3, 1878, pp. 141-144, 283-289.

Mill, John Stuart.
——*Political Writings of.* Boston Review, by J. H. Ward, vol. 6, 1866, pp. 567-590.

——*Portrait by Watts, etched by Rajon.* Portfolio, by P. G. Hamerton, 1875, p. 11.

——*Relations with Mrs. Taylor.* Overland Monthly, by S. E. Henshaw, vol. 13, 1874, pp. 516-523.

——*Religious Confessions of.* Eclectic Magazine (from the Spectator), vol. 21 N.S., 1875, pp. 108-111; same article, Littell's Living Age, vol. 123, pp. 508-512.

——*Religious Philosophy of.* International Review, by N. Porter, vol. 2, 1875, pp. 540-562.

——*Reminiscence of.* Victoria Magazine, by C. L. Brace, vol. 21, 1873, pp. 265-270.

——*School of.* Quarterly Review, vol. 133, 1872, pp. 77-118.

——*Writings of.* Christian Examiner, by C. A. Cummings, vol. 74, 1863, pp. 1-43.—British Quarterly Review, vol. 48, 1868, pp. 1-58; same article, Eclectic Magazine, vol. 19 N.S., 1874, pp. 580-591.

IV. CHRONOLOGICAL LIST OF WORKS.

Printed by WALTER SCOTT, *Felling, Newcastle-on-Tyne.*

www.ingramcontent.com/pod-product-compliance
Lightning Source LLC
Chambersburg PA
CBHW032007060726

47497CB00017B/2361